MANHATTAN HIT MAN

A TANNER NOVEL - BOOK 18

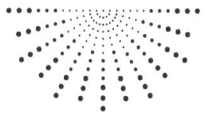

REMINGTON KANE

Year Zero

INTRODUCTION

MANHATTAN HIT MAN – A TANNER NOVEL – BOOK 18

Tanner returns to New York City and becomes involved in a war as the Boston mob makes moves to take over New York City.

Meanwhile, after Sara agrees to do a favor for an old friend things turn deadly, and she finds herself fighting for her life.

ACKNOWLEDGMENTS

I write for you.

—Remington Kane

1
NEW YORK, NEW YORK

Tanner slammed his car door shut to avoid being struck by a red Corvette with numerous chips and cracks in its fiberglass body. As the car sped past him, its passenger gave him the finger.

Tanner was on the FDR Drive and headed into Manhattan when the pickup truck in front of him bounced in and out of a deep pothole. That caused an old wooden sawhorse to tumble out of the pickup's rear. The sawhorse broke into pieces from the impact and blocked the lane. Tanner had come to a stop to avoid running into it, while the cars behind him followed suit.

Meanwhile, the driver of the pickup truck seemed oblivious to what had occurred and just kept driving.

After putting his flashers on, Tanner told Sara he'd be right back and opened his door to step out and move the debris to the side of the road to clear the lane, which was the right lane. Meanwhile, the left lane, which was free of debris, continued to move along at a steady pace, as did the traffic on the other side of the highway.

The punk in the red Corvette, driving several car

lengths behind Tanner, cursed the stopped traffic in front of him and risked getting in the path of a speeding dump truck in the left lane. Before the dump truck could collide with his rear, the Corvette driver dived back into the right lane, nearly sideswiping Tanner.

Tanner had placed one foot on the roadway. Hearing the pitch of the Corvette's racing motor, he yanked his foot back in the car and closed the door just in time to see the Corvette come within inches of hitting his rental. Had Tanner's reflexes been any slower, he might have been struck and dragged along the highway.

The punk driving the Corvette did not possess good reflexes. He stood on the brake pedal when he saw the broken sawhorse lying in the right lane, but it was too late. The Corvette ran over the debris, sending sparks flying from the nails in the wood, as they scraped along the road surface. Then came the sound of a blown tire, and the once proud but abused car skidded to a halt, blocking the lane. As he thundered by the scene, the driver of the dump truck blew his air horn and kept going.

Sara placed a hand on Tanner's shoulder. "Are you all right?"

"I'm good."

Sara looked at the Corvette. "Are those the same two from the airport?"

"That's them," Tanner said.

They had first encountered the punks while at the airport. The two men, both in their thirties, were harassing every good-looking woman they came across by ogling them. Any females that didn't meet their high standards were pointed at, whispered about, and subjected to their laughter.

Most of the women, like Sara, just ignored the fools, but there was an overweight woman in the airport terminal who cried silent tears after they laughed at her. Their whispered, but still audible, comment about how she was a, "Fat chick," was followed by the idiots making pig sounds.

The fortyish woman in question was beautiful, well-dressed, and exuded intelligence, while the Neanderthals making fun of her wore ragged jeans and jackets that had seen better days. They were also far from being perfect physical specimens themselves, as both men had the beginning of a beer belly.

The next encounter Tanner and Sara had with the fools occurred as they were leaving the airport. The driver of the Corvette, a man with dark hair and a bushy moustache cursed at Tanner and blew his horn in anger.

Tanner had made it in front of a slow tractor-trailer, while the Corvette driver was stuck behind the huge vehicle. That was the last Tanner had seen of the Vette until it came close to striking him.

The driver and passenger jumped from the car and sent a string of obscenities into the air when they saw what they had run over. Along with the flat tire, fluid was leaking out from beneath the vehicle.

Both men looked up from the mess to stare at Tanner, then began walking toward him.

Tanner smiled. "It looks like they want to play."

"Don't kill them. They're just idiots."

"I won't even touch them unless they get physical first."

Tanner left his car and met the two punks in front of the hood. They were both big men, the driver with his bushy black moustache, and his passenger, who had long blond hair that was greasy.

Moustache pointed at Tanner while scowling. "Why didn't you warn me that shit was in the road? Look what happened to my ride."

"Shut up and go back to your car," Tanner said.

Long hair moved closer and leaned in, while giving Tanner what he must have thought was an intimidating stare. "Who you talkin' to, asshole?"

"I was talking to your friend, but the same goes for you. Shut your mouth, turn around, and walk away."

Long hair glanced at Moustache, as a smile curled his lips. "You hear this shit?"

"I hear it, and the fucker is looking for an ass-kicking."

Tanner smiled as well. They were two to his one, had twenty pounds apiece on him, and he had an arm in a splint from an injury still healing from a fight he'd recently had in Russia.

To the left, in the other lane, traffic was moving along in a hesitant manner. The drivers of the vehicles were slowing down to look at them and the damaged sports car. Beyond that was the other side of the highway, which was bordered by the East River. The river looked gray and flat, as the day offered scant wind and an overcast sky.

One of the cars pulled out of the flow of traffic and stopped in front of the Corvette. The vehicle had a tinted rear window, so Tanner couldn't get a look at the driver. He hoped it wasn't a friend of the two dolts standing before him, and doubted it was. The car was a late-model Mercedes whose owner had taste. Whoever was inside the car seemed content to just sit and watch the show.

Moustache pointed at Tanner with a finger that was an inch shy of touching his chest.

"I see you got a jacked-up arm. If you don't want a face to match, give me some money to get my car fixed."

"Pay for your own stupidity," Tanner said.

The pointing finger jabbed at him. "Who you calling stupid?"

Tanner placed a foot behind the man's ankle, reached up, and yanked hard on one side of the moustache. The punk stumbled backwards several feet, lost his balance, and landed on his ass. Long hair watched his friend go down, then took a wild swing at Tanner's face. Tanner ducked the blow easily and brought a knee up into the man's stomach. That caused Long hair to bend over. Tanner smashed a fist into the side of his head, and Long hair fell onto the roadway like someone stole his bones.

Moustache rose from the ground and charged at Tanner with his head down, as if to tackle him. Tanner waited until the last instant before stepping aside, then watched as Moustache tried to change direction. The attempt failed, and Moustache collided against the front of Tanner's rental. Before he could recover, Tanner sent a booted foot into his face that broke the man's nose. Moustache straightened as his hands flew to his face, but Tanner's second kick caught the punk on the chin and sent him sprawling. Moustache settled on the blacktop beside his friend, and like his friend, he was unconscious.

The door opened on the car that had pulled over in front of the Corvette. When Tanner saw the driver of the vehicle, he recognized her. It was the woman from the airport. The overweight one whom the men had teased and ridiculed. She walked over and stared down at the two idiots. There was a stun gun in her right hand. When she looked up at Tanner, he saw she was smiling.

"Thank you for teaching them a lesson. I wish I could have done it myself."

"It was a pleasure," Tanner said.

The woman held up the stun gun. "I was going to use this on them if they hurt you, but I see I didn't need it."

Tanner said nothing to that, nodded at the woman, and turned to get back in the car.

"Sir?"

Tanner gave her a quizzical look as he placed a hand on the door handle. "Yes?"

"What's your name?"

Tanner answered her by using his assumed name. "I'm Thomas Myers."

"Thomas, my name is Martha Maglione. I own a restaurant in the city that my father started, it's called Maglione's. Have you heard of it?"

Tanner nodded again. Maglione's was famous for its Italian cuisine, along with the fact that many Broadway stars dined there. Tanner had eaten there once when his dinner companion had been Sophia Verona.

"Come by anytime and I'll feed you and your lady there for free," Martha Maglione said.

"Thanks, we might take you up on that."

A moan came from behind Martha. It was Moustache. He sat up and looked around with a dazed expression. Martha pressed the stun gun to his forehead and pulled the trigger. Moustache jerked, writhed in a spastic fashion, then fell onto his back and drooled.

Martha smiled at Tanner. "That was fun."

2
THIS IS A JOKE, RIGHT?

Hours later, Tanner and Sara stood outside the new strip club named Johnny R's.

The club was built on the same property where once sat the Cabaret Strip Club. That club had been owned and operated by the late Johnny Rossetti, while the new club bore his name as a tribute.

Joe Pullo bought the land where an abandoned factory had sat across the street from the old club. The factory was torn down and a restaurant and dance club were in its place. An enclosed pedestrian bridge over the road connected that property to Johnny R's invitation-only VIP section, while regular customers entered from street level.

Purple and blue neon lettering announced the strip club's presence and purpose. Their light reflected off streets wet from an afternoon rain shower. The sound of rock music came from the club every time a new patron entered, usually accompanied by the men's laughter.

Whether they realized it or not, the mirth was directed at themselves. They were grown men spending hard-earned dollars to ogle women while drinking overpriced drinks. The women made money, the club owners made money, but the men left the clubs poorer, inebriated, titillated, but feeling perhaps just a little sad. But then, all fantasies have costs, while most deliver little more than promises.

Tanner searched Sara's face and saw a look of apprehension. "You don't have to be here, Sara. I could talk to Joe alone."

"No, I owe Joe a personal apology for the damage I caused. Johnny's death was my fault and I have to live with it."

"He may not accept that apology."

"I know, but I also want him to see that I've changed, and that we're together as a couple."

"Why is that important to you?"

"He's your friend, Tanner. I want to get along with your friends."

"I would like that too. Let's go see where we stand."

They entered the club, and an impressive sight met their eyes. The new club was larger than the old. There were huge monitors hanging from the ceiling, and they showed the dancers at twice their normal size. On stage, blonde twins danced for the patrons and the crowd looked on with rapt attention.

Tanner tore his gaze away to take in another impressive set of twins. They were the bouncers who worked the door. The two black men were tall, wide, and packed with muscle. By Tanner's estimate, they would each tip the scale at over three hundred pounds. They had been searching the club for signs of trouble, bouncers looking for prey to bounce on. The two men met Tanner's intense eyes with deadpan expressions, but then seemed to tense as they gave each other warning glances. They recognized a fellow predator when they saw one.

They wore their hair short, but their beards were full, below their hazel eyes.

"Can we help you?" the one on the left said.

"My name is Tanner. Joe Pullo is expecting me."

Smiles brightened the giants' faces, and the one on the left stepped closer.

"Mr. Pullo asked that we show you to the office, Mr. Tanner. You and the lady please follow me, sir."

The man led them past the dance floor where the other set of twins were showing how flexible they could be while hanging upside down. As they passed the bar, Tanner nodded to a familiar face that smiled a greeting to him. It was a bartender named Carl, who had worked at the old Cabaret Strip Club. Tanner liked Carl, but Carl's smile looked more worried than pleasant. It likely meant nothing, as Carl was the nervous type.

Tanner and Sara followed the bouncer onto an elevator that required a four-digit code to enter. Tanner saw that the rear wall of the elevator was another set of doors. It was how Joe came and went from the club. After rising a flight, they stepped into a posh but small reception area where a desk sat devoid of its receptionist. The room was soundproofed, but you could still feel the vibration of the music that throbbed beneath you.

Although the reception desk was unoccupied, there was someone seated on a sofa to the left of the desk, near a door marked, STAIRS. The man was so large that he dwarfed the bouncer.

"Hello, Big Ralphie," Tanner said.

"Hey there, Tanner, long time no see, you too, Miss Blake."

"See you around," Tanner said.

A knock on the right side of twin oak doors was answered by the voice of Joe Pullo. As the bouncer opened the door, Tanner reached over and took Sara's hand. Her palm was moist, indicating her nervousness. Sara gripped his hand, offered a smile, and the two of them walked into an office with a glass wall made of one-way mirrors that looked down on the club.

There was a wooden desk gleaming before the window. The desk was as long as a car and likely as expensive. The chair behind it was thickly padded and covered in leather, while the right wall contained a wet bar, along with four stools.

Joe Pullo, Don of the Giacconi Crime Family, was seated on a long black leather sofa that took up the left side of the room. Joe's wife, Laurel, was with him, and Tanner displayed his surprise when he realized she was pregnant, and well along by the size of her. His hosts wore their own surprised looks, although, a better description might be to describe their expressions as shocked. They were staring at Tanner and Sara's entwined hands.

The bouncer ended the growing silence. "Is it all good, boss?"

"Yeah, Robert, and thanks."

"I'm Michael, the good-looking one."

"I should make you two wear name tags," Joe said.

The bouncer left without comment after Joe rose from the sofa. Joe was grinning as he approached Tanner to shake his hand.

"You've become a damned legend since the last time I saw you," Joe looked over at Sara. "And I see you're still full of surprises."

Laurel got up from the sofa with a touch of difficulty and approached them with a mouth opened in shock. Seeing her expression, Sara released Tanner's hand.

Laurel gaped at Tanner, then Sara, and shook her head

in disbelief. "This is a joke, right, Tanner? Please tell me you and this witch are not involved."

"Hello Laurel, I see you're keeping company with someone new as well."

Laurel relaxed as she looked down at herself. "Yes, Joe and I are having a baby."

Tanner raised an eyebrow as he looked at Joe. "A boy?"

Joe beamed with pride. "Yeah, I'm gonna have a son."

Tanner smiled, but it faded as Laurel moved closer and stared up at him.

"Are you and Sara Blake together?"

"Yes, Laurel."

"Tanner, the woman stuck a gun in my mouth and threatened to pull the trigger. Now you're sleeping with her?"

"Sara's different now."

"Laurel," Sara said.

Laurel looked at her with eyes filled with venom. "What?"

"I apologize for everything I did to you and I truly am sorry."

"I don't want an apology. I want to never see you again."

"Are you saying we're not welcome here?" Tanner asked.

Joe put an arm around his wife's shoulders. "She's not saying that, are you, Laurel?"

Laurel's gaze softened as she looked at her husband. When she stared at Sara again, it was accompanied by a sigh. "Tanner is always welcome here, and… so are you… for as long as you two last."

Sara's smile was tentative. "Thank you… I think."

Laurel took out her phone. "Joe, I'm going to text the chauffeur. I want to go home and sleep."

"All right, baby, and tell Red to drive slow."

"He does, in fact, he crawls along since I became pregnant. I think he's afraid I'll go into labor and he'll have to deliver the baby."

"I don't think I know anyone named Red," Tanner said.

Joe smiled. "The kid is Russian. He was Michael Krupin's driver."

"One of Krupin's men is driving your wife around?"

"Yeah, but the kid's all right."

"Can he handle himself if there's trouble?"

Joe laughed. "Red is strictly a driver, but Big Ralphie never leaves Laurel's side. Anyway, I'll tell you the story later."

Laurel hugged Tanner, then kissed him on the cheek. "It's so good to have you back in the city. Please tell me you'll be staying."

"I will, as soon as Sara and I find an apartment."

"I can help you there," Joe said.

After getting a return text saying the limo was ready, Laurel kissed Joe goodbye and headed for the elevator. As she was closing the office door, Laurel sent a cold stare toward Sara.

"Well, Laurel hates me, is that true for you as well, Joe?"

"I won't lie, honey, you're not my favorite person, not after what happened to Johnny Rossetti."

Sara's eyes grew moist. "I loved Johnny, and it was my misplaced hatred for Tanner that caused his death. I live with that every day, Joe, believe me I do."

Joe stared at Sara for long moments, then, he gestured at the two of them, as he pointed at Sara's knee brace and Tanner's arm splint.

"Did you two do that to each other?"

Tanner looked down at his arm. "I received this from a fight I had with a Russian revolutionary during a blizzard. Sara's injury came from a plane crash after we'd been shot down in Siberia."

"You two aren't boring, I'll say that for you. Now, how about a drink?"

Sara declined a drink, as she was meeting her sister at a bar soon, but Tanner had a beer. They settled together on the long sofa with Sara sitting at Tanner's right and to the left of Joe.

"How is Sammy doing these days, Joe?" Tanner asked.

"Physically, he's gold, but that kid hasn't been the same since Sophia died. There's no joy in him anymore, Tanner. No lie, that boy hasn't smiled once since Sophia was killed, and the kid was always the happy type."

"What's he doing?"

Joe chuckled. "He's following in his grandfather's footsteps. Sammy's my main enforcer. That's how Sam got his start, hell, me too, and Sammy is as good as I was."

"And do you need my help?"

"Maybe."

Sara kissed Tanner on the cheek, then stood. "I'll be going now, Joe. I'm meeting my sister in Midtown."

Joe nodded at Sara, but he didn't rise from the sofa.

Tanner rose, kissed Sara, and told her he'd see her later.

"If you need a taxi, there's always at least one in front of the club," Joe said. "You know, to pour the drunks into."

Sara moved her hand around, in a gesture that encompassed the whole building. "Johnny would have liked this, Joe. I think he'd be honored that you named it after him, and that he's not forgotten."

"It's the least I could do, Sara. I failed to protect him."

Sara made a pained expression. "You share no responsibility in his death. That's my cross to bear."

Joe studied her. "You really loved Johnny, didn't you?"

"Yes, and now I care for Tanner. I hope someday you'll accept that."

"What the hell, if Tanner can live and let live after all the shit you put him through, I guess I can too. Now Laurel, that's a different story."

"I'll avoid her. She shouldn't be upset during her pregnancy, and congratulations on having a son. Have you picked a name yet?"

Joe's smile was bittersweet. "He'll be named Johnny."

3

RED, FED, AND DEAD

After Sara left to meet her sister, Joe brought Tanner up to speed about what was happening in New York.

"Business is good, as usual, but we've been hit twice over the last few weeks by a heist crew."

"You've been hit? You mean the Giacconi Family?"

"Yeah, a drug shipment: two tons of weed, and then a hijacked truck filled with flat screen TV's was taken from the guys who stole it in the first place. Let me tell you, that was embarrassing."

"It sounds like an inside job."

"Oh yeah, and we're looking into it."

"Any suspects?"

"Three of them, Red, Fed, and Dead."

"What?"

Joe laughed. "Red is the kid I talked about earlier. He's our chauffeur. It's not him. The kid isn't the type, and he'd do anything for me."

"Why?"

"Once Michael Krupin died and the Alvarado cartel

took over, Rico Nazario went on a purge in that office building they had. When it came time to ice Krupin's chauffeur, I saved the kid's life."

"Why?"

"His real name is Andre, and he's no gangster. He only took the gig of driving Krupin around because it was his late father's job and the family needed the money."

"The kid's father was killed during the war with the Russians?"

"Nah, he wasn't a soldier either. He died of lung cancer."

Tanner studied Joe. "There's something else. There must be, or you wouldn't trust the kid."

"You're right. He saved me. One of Krupin's thugs was hiding up in the duct work. Once we thought they were all dead, the guy came out of hiding. Red tackled me to the ground as the guy took a shot at me. Bosco killed the bastard, but Red took one in the shoulder. After that, I made Red my driver."

"All right, that leaves Fed and Dead."

"You know who Fed is, it's Tamir Ivanov."

"The FBI man who killed Krupin? He works for you?"

"He retired, became bored, then asked for a job when I opened up this place. He's the manager of Johnny R's. The guy grew up in his old man's bar, and he's a natural with the girls."

Tanner wore a smirk. "I'm almost afraid to ask who Dead is."

"You know him too."

"Who is it?"

"Rico Nazario."

"Joe, part of the reason I killed Alvarado was so you could get rid of Rico."

"I know, but the bastard is good at what he does. The

jobs that are too big for Sammy to handle are passed off to Rico and his crew."

"You gave him a crew?"

"All guys I've known since forever. They all vouch for Rico and were with him at the times we were hit."

"But you still don't trust him, or do you?"

"Hell no, Tanner, that bastard is on probation forever. The thing is, before you killed Alvarado, Rico could have made life hell for me. He didn't though. I remembered that when the tables were turned."

"You mind if I kill him?"

"You dislike him that much?"

"It was a joke, like calling him Dead."

Joe smiled. "That nickname makes for a good reminder of how thin the ice is he's skating on."

"Now, about those bouncers?"

"Robert and Michael, what about them?"

Tanner grinned. "They don't look Italian."

Joe waved a hand at that. "That was Sam's rule. I just look to hire the best, and those two came highly recommended from Philly."

"Any other surprises?"

"Not really, but Johnny's kid sister is home after finishing college in L.A. Her name is Gina and she's a knockout."

"Any chance of her and Sammy hooking up?"

"I wish, but all Sammy ever does is work."

"Is that where he is now?"

"Sammy is visiting a late payer who owes us some big stacks, and get this, the guy lives on Park Avenue."

"Is Sammy visiting the guy to remind him of his responsibilities, or is he visiting the guy to break his legs?"

"Legs, the sonofabitch owes nearly three-hundred grand."

"And Sammy is good at the work?"

Joe shrugged. "It takes his mind off losing Sophia, and losing that girl hardened him."

"He's young, he'll find another woman to give a damn about someday."

"I hope you're right, and look at me, married and soon to be a father. I never saw it coming."

"Sara's been a surprise too."

Joe cocked his head. "You two are serious?"

"Like you said, I never saw it coming."

"Well, I'll be damned."

Tanner laughed. "That makes two of us."

ON PARK AVENUE, SAMMY GIACCONI STOOD IN THE FOYER of a luxury condo. It was owned by a man named Chase Rawlins. Rawlins was forty-six, a graduate of Princeton, and the owner of his own brokerage firm. He was also seconds away from experiencing more pain than he could imagine.

"But I paid!" Rawlins said. "I gave the money to that other man, Valente."

"Ricky Valente doesn't collect at this level. That's why you're dealing with me now," Sammy said.

Sammy's suit was as finely-tailored as Rawlins was, and it fit his lean frame well. Sammy's hair, which had always been worn long, was much shorter. The eyes, always so full of mischief and youthful exuberance, were cold, and looked older than the face they sat in.

"Mr. Giacconi, I swear to you I paid every damn cent. Look around, see the empty walls? I sold my wife's art collection to get that money, some vacant land too. I paid. I swear I paid."

Sammy stared at Rawlins. The man seemed sincere, and why should he lie about something that was so easy to confirm? Sammy took out his phone and called Ricky Valente. There was no answer, so he left a message.

"When did you pay Valente?"

"Today. He came by my office and said he was there to collect. I didn't have it there, of course, so we returned here and I gave him the money from the safe."

"Come with me," Sammy said.

"Wh… where?"

"Relax, we're just going down to talk with building security. If Valente was here they'd have a record of it. There are cameras in the lobby and in the elevators."

"Yes!" Rawlins cried. "Yes, and that will prove I'm not lying."

"We'll see," Sammy said.

TEN MINUTES LATER, SAMMY WAS LOOKING AT VIDEO OF Ricky Valente that was recorded in the building that afternoon. Valente was a large man in his early-forties with curly brown hair. When Ricky Valente left Chase Rawlins' apartment, he was clutching a laptop case and wearing a smile.

Sammy sighed. The dumb bastard had stolen from them.

Rawlins looked at Sammy with a worried gaze. "Is that proof enough for you?"

"Yeah, consider yourself paid up."

The relief on Rawlins' face was palpable, while Sammy's face had reddened from the anger he was feeling.

"Did Valente say anything while he was with you? What did you two talk about?"

"Nothing really. Thinking back on it, he was as nervous as I was."

"He should be more nervous now. If you hear from him, give us a call."

"Oh, yeah, and listen, Mr. Giacconi, I may need to borrow again soon, just a little. It all depends on what my accountant says I owe the tax man."

Sammy stared at Rawlins. Some people never learned.

However, Ricky Valente would learn a lesson about stealing from the wrong people, and it would be his last lesson.

4
THIS IS A JOKE, RIGHT? – PART 2

Sara smiled as her sister Jennifer wrapped her in a huge hug of greeting.

Jennifer was a newlywed, having recently married Sara's ex-partner from her days in the FBI, Jake Garner. Jennifer was several years older than Sara and was a blonde. The blonde hair was shining beneath the lights of the pub they were meeting in and was worn shoulder-length.

When Jennifer released Sara, she pointed down at Sara's left leg. "Oh, it's so good to see you, but what happened to your knee?"

"I suffered trauma to a ligament. The brace comes off in a few days, but then I have to do certain exercises for several weeks."

"That doesn't sound too serious, but how did you hurt it?"

Sara wasn't about to tell her sister the truth, that she and Tanner had been shot out of the sky by a group of mercenaries and crashed onto a frozen lake in Siberia. Jennifer had always been motherly toward her younger sister. If she knew how close Sara came to dying, it would only worry her.

"I slipped on ice and hit my knee on something, and you're right, it's not a serious injury. Now, tell me all about your honeymoon."

Jennifer grinned. "I can do better than that. I have pictures."

THE TWO SISTERS CAUGHT UP OVER DRINKS, MARTINIS FOR Sara, and white wine for Jennifer. When Sara thought the time was right, she brought up the subject of Tanner, or rather, Jennifer asked a question that would bring their relationship out in the open.

"You're seeing someone, aren't you?"

"As a matter of fact, I am."

"I thought so. What's he like?"

"Well… I once thought of him as the worst sort of human being, but after getting to know him… I, well I… I think I love him."

Jennifer tilted her head to one side as her lips parted in surprise. "Love? Who is this guy?"

"Jenny, I'm talking about Tanner. He and I are together now."

Sara waited for a reaction, but Jennifer just stared at her with a blank expression.

"Jenny? Jenny, say something."

Jennifer let out a gasp, swallowed the remainder of her drink in a gulp, then released a sigh.

"I was happy when you moved on from your obsessive hatred for the man, but if you're with Tanner, perhaps your obsession with him has just taken a different form, a dramatically different form. I mean, seriously, are you two really lovers?"

Sara felt herself growing angry, but she dispersed it with a long exhale of breath. She could understand Jennifer's reasoning, as well as her concerns.

"I was obsessed with paying Tanner back for killing Brian, yes, but I've gotten over that. As you once pointed out to me, Brian was no saint. He was killed by Tanner as a direct result of the choices he made."

Jennifer looked surprised again. "You blame Brian for the fact that Tanner killed him?"

"Brian was responsible for the series of events that brought Tanner to him. There are consequences that come with the life Brian was leading. Tanner was one of those consequences."

"Tanner risked his life to save me last year, but Sara, the man is still a paid assassin. How can you be with someone like that?"

"When Tanner and I rescued you last year, that was when I began to see him as a person. Tanner is not a heartless killer, a highly trained assassin, yes, but not a heartless killer. He has his own sorrows in his past, and he has more heart, more compassion than I ever would have imagined. And surprisingly, he has one hell of a good sense of humor."

For several tense seconds, the two sisters stared at each other without speaking. Then, Jennifer broke the silence with a question.

"What do you want me to say, that I'm happy for you?"

"You don't need to say anything, just know that I'm happy, and I'm with someone who cares for me and understands me."

"Do you really love him?"

"Yes."

"Does he know that?"

"I think so, and I think he loves me, although, we haven't said the actual words yet."

Jennifer made a small sound of laughter. "I'm at a loss as to what to say here. On one hand, I'm overjoyed that you've found someone, but on the other hand, I feel dread for what the future may bring. Jake tells me that Tanner lives a dangerous life."

"He does face danger on a regular basis, yes, but then, so does Jake, am I right?"

Jennifer made a face. "Don't remind me. Jake was shot at recently when he tracked down a terror suspect with his team of agents."

"It seems we both have men who aren't afraid of danger."

"But they're on different sides of the law."

"True, but don't forget, Tanner helped Jake get his promotion by giving him that informant in the Chemzonic case."

"I know, but I still don't understand why Tanner helped him."

"Tanner is a complicated man, but my guess is that he likes Jake. The two of them managed to get along when we all worked together in Guambi to save you from those terrorists."

"Jake was impressed with Tanner, and he's grateful for his help."

Sara hesitated for a moment, as she was uncertain of the reaction she would receive.

"I want you and Tanner to meet. You're the two most important people in my life and I would love it if you two could at least be civil to each other."

"I've already met Tanner, and why wouldn't I be civil to the man?"

"You weren't civil toward Johnny Rossetti when you met him. In fact, you insulted him."

Jennifer winced at the reminder of how she had behaved. "You caught me off-guard by being with a mobster, although, I shouldn't have been, you always did like the bad boys."

"Is that a yes? Will you meet with me and Tanner over drinks?"

"I'll go you one better and invite you two to dinner, but it will have to wait a week or so. Jake is in DC for several days, then he has to attend a training seminar in San Diego. I'll be going with him to San Diego."

Sara grinned. "Dinner it is, and thank you, Jenny. It means a lot to me that you're willing to accept Tanner."

"The man saved my life. I can at least be polite to him."

Sara leaned back in her seat and sighed. "Breaking this news to you went better than I thought."

"There's a reason for that."

"What reason?"

Jennifer reached across the table and took Sara's hand. "You look as happy as I've ever seen you."

Sara gave a little shrug. "I'm in love."

"With Tanner," Jennifer said, and the words were laced with astonishment.

5
MEANWHILE, BACK IN KILLBURRY

Sammy entered an apartment in the East Village that was a few blocks away from Tompkins Square Park. The apartment belonged to Ricky Valente. After knocking several times, Sammy tried the doorknob and it turned. The door had been left unlocked.

Sammy reached inside and flicked the lights on, as his other hand took out his gun. The apartment looked normal. There was a matching sofa and love seat, a coffee table, and a large TV bolted to a wall. In the bedroom, Sammy came across evidence that Ricky had fled.

The closet door sat open and there were gaps along the rod that held Ricky's clothing. In the bathroom, toiletries were missing, such as a toothbrush, toothpaste, and deodorant. The apartment's tiny kitchen had a sink filled with dirty dishes and cups, while the garbage can overflowed with trash.

Perhaps Ricky always lived like a slob. Then again, maybe he saw no point in cleaning dishes and emptying the garbage since he knew he was leaving and never coming back.

Sammy checked the building's underground parking garage and found Ricky's car, a small green Ford he used to make collections. That meant he was smart enough to leave the city in something different, a vehicle that the Giacconi Family wouldn't be able to track.

Before leaving, Sammy broke into Ricky's mailbox in the lobby. The mailbox was one among thirty-six brass rectangular slots and had Ricky's last name adhered to it on a red label. The building didn't have a doorman, but it did have a camera in a corner of the ceiling. Sammy severed the wire that powered the camera and used a screwdriver he'd taken from Ricky's car to pop open the mailbox.

After emptying the contents of the mail slot, Sammy walked out of the building and returned to his car. He drove until he found a parking space, pulled over, and began going through Ricky's mail.

It consisted mainly of bills, but there were two notes from the building management. Ricky hadn't been paying his rent and was on the verge of facing legal action. Ricky had stopped paying his bills because he knew he wouldn't be around to face any flack that came from being a deadbeat. This told Sammy that Valente's decision to steal from them hadn't been made on the spur of the moment, but had been planned far in advance. Chase Rawlins' huge payment just made the timing more advantageous.

Sammy grabbed his phone and checked the file that held the list of payments Valente would have collected during the day. The list was encrypted, and the names were indecipherable without a code key, but the amounts they owed could be figured out by moving each digit two spaces to the left and multiplying by seven. Sammy wrote down the numbers on the back of one of Valente's unpaid bills and came up with a total. $348,800.00

That was how much Ricky Valente had run off with. It was also the amount of money he would die over. Sammy planned to track Valente down, and once he did, Ricky Valente would learn that you don't steal from the Giacconis.

Sammy lowered the passenger window on his car, leaned across the seat, and dropped Valente's mail in a trashcan. After putting the car in gear, he headed toward Johnny R's, to give the news of Ricky's betrayal to Joe Pullo.

AT THAT VERY MOMENT INSIDE JOHNNY R'S, JOE WAS telling Tanner about another thief. The crime syndicate calling themselves the Brotherhood had entered the town of Killburry, Connecticut, and killed Burt Hodges. Hodges had been the Giacconi's man in Killburry. Tanner, who'd been living in Killburry at the time, destroyed the Brotherhood, but before Joe could send a new man there to replace Hodges, the Boston mob made a move on the town.

"That sounds like an act of war," Tanner said.

"It is, and I'm wondering if Boston is following it up with these heists we've had."

"Who runs things up there?"

"A guy named Moss Murphy. He's a little older than me and has a son about Sammy's age. The son, Liam Murphy, he's the one that moved into Killburry."

"Ah, I see. If you had sent a crew up to take back Killburry you'd have been killing one of Murphy's family. Is that why you haven't retaliated?"

"That's it, but we both know that I can't let things stand either. For now, I'm just watching and waiting."

"Waiting for what?"

"These heists, I need to know if they're connected to Boston or something else altogether. Once I know that, I'll make a move."

"You don't want to fight a war on two fronts if you can avoid it?"

"Exactly."

"What's the Boston mob like?"

"Moss Murphy is a weasel, but he's a smart weasel. His number two man is a guy named Finn Kelly. Kelly doesn't look like much, but I've heard he's as good as they come. Now Liam, the son, he's nothing but a punk. Moss tried to keep him out of the business by sending him off to college, same as Sam tried to keep Sammy out, but hey, once they're men, they're men."

"It sounds like Liam Murphy may not live long enough to become an old man."

"I'd have whacked him already if he wasn't Moss's boy, and Moss knows that the kid did wrong. Killburry hardly made any money for us and it sure as hell isn't worth starting a war over."

"But that's what it will come to, it's just a matter of when."

"First, we stop this heist crew, then I'll take Killburry back. I'll do it in such a way that leaves Liam Murphy in one piece."

Tanner sat his beer bottle on the coffee table and stood. "Let me know if you need help. Until then, I'll just be waiting around for my arm to heal."

Joe stood and took Tanner by the shoulders. "I meant what I said earlier, you've become a damn legend on the streets. Taking out a drug cartel leader was badass enough, but killing Maurice Scallato cinched it. Watch your back,

Tanner. There are punks out there that will take a crack at you in the hope of gaining a rep."

"There's a name for people like that."

"What is it?"

"Dead."

Joe laughed. "Welcome back, buddy. It's good to have you home."

6

A FOUR-LETTER WORD

TWO DAYS LATER, TANNER, WITH SARA BESIDE HIM, DROVE his car onto the driveway that led to their lake property. They were both pleased to see that everything looked the same. Their two massive RVs gleamed in the sun. Tanner's was blue and white, while Sara's, which sat across the lake, was green and white. Other than their color, they were identical.

As Tanner parked near the shack on the property, the caretakers emerged. They were Pete and Rocco, two brothers that Tanner had met when he lived in Killburry. Pete and Rocco would never score high on an IQ test, but the boys were all heart and loyal.

Tanner had endeared himself to the boys when he saved them from a pair of punks that were out to kill them. They were then left in charge of the lakefront property while Tanner and Sara were off hunting down Maurice Scallato. They knew Sara by her real name, but called Tanner by his alias, Tom Myers.

Rocco raced from the shack with a huge grin on his face and charged at Tanner. He stopped short, with a mouth forming an O, when he saw that Tanner's left arm was in a splint.

"What happened, Tom Myers? Did you break your arm?"

"Sort of, but it will heal."

Rocco pointed at Sara's knee brace. "Did you break your knee?"

Sara grinned at him. "Not exactly."

Rocco smiled at them. "Welcome home, Tom Myers and Sara Blake."

Sara kissed Rocco on the cheek, then watched him blush, as his brother, Pete, joined them.

"We took good care of the RVs, Mr. Myers. We even cleaned the snow off them last week."

"That's good, Pete, how have you two been doing?"

"We're good. We like it here, but we'll be happy when spring comes and we can use the lake again."

"It's too cold now," Rocco said.

"How's the heat in that shack?" Sara asked.

Pete made a face. "It's chilly in there at night."

"Use my RV. I'll be moving in with Mr. Myers."

Rocco's eyes grew large. "Are you serious, Sara Blake? We can live in the green RV?"

"Move in whenever you're ready, and take good care of it."

"We will," Pete and Rocco answered at the same time.

Sara stopped by the green motor home to gather her things. There wasn't much, as she kept an apartment in Connecticut that she planned to leave. She had only owned the RV for a few weeks before they left the lake and hadn't many belongings there.

Tanner was never the talkative sort, but it seemed to Sara that he had grown quieter than usual. As he opened the trunk to carry her things inside his RV, Sara placed a hand on his arm.

"Was this presumptuous of me?"

"What do you mean? Your moving in here?"

"I realize now that we never talked about it and that I simply assumed it was what you wanted too."

"You weren't wrong," Tanner said.

They carried her things inside. When Sara opened the closet in the bedroom, there were several items of women's clothing already there, a dress, two blouses, and a pair of shoes.

"Those belonged to Alexa," Tanner said. "She didn't have room for them when she left."

He was sitting on the bed. Sara sat beside him and leaned her head on his shoulder.

"Do you miss her?"

"I did, before you, but no, not anymore."

"Tell me if I'm moving too fast for you. I know you, Tanner. You've spent most of your life living alone."

"That changed with Alexa, but even before that, Laurel made me realize that I needed someone."

"Then why didn't you stay with Laurel?"

Tanner sighed. "Fear. Loving her scared me, because I didn't want to need her. I didn't want to need anyone."

"Because of what happened to your family?"

"You understand that?"

"I do. But we all need someone, and Alexa broke through your defenses."

"And then she left me alone."

Sara pushed gently on Tanner's chest until they were both lying back on the bed with their feet still touching the floor. She turned her head and looked at him.

"I love you."

"I…I…love you."

Sara laughed. "Did that hurt coming out?"

"It is a word filled with pain."

"And promise, the word love is filled with promise too."

Tanner stared at her. "How did we ever get here?"

"We survived each other."

"You despised me, now you say you love me. How does that work?"

Sara kissed him. "It's called a miracle, baby."

Tanner caressed her face. "Where do we go from here?"

"We take it one day at a time and see what happens."

"It's been my experience that love only brings pain."

"That's the end of love, not love itself."

"Maybe."

Sara smiled. "We make quite a pair. Every man I've ever loved has died and your relationships always end."

Tanner made a sour face. "That doesn't inspire confidence."

"It does if you think about it."

"What do you mean?"

"You know that when I set my mind to something I don't stop until I get it, regardless of the risks or the odds."

"Like my head on a chopping block?"

"Yes. I'm not proud of the way I used Laurel against you, but it did finally place you at my mercy. Meanwhile, there's no one harder to kill than yourself. So, think about it. I know you won't die on me and you can trust me not to give up on us."

Tanner looked thoughtful, then let out a long laugh.

"What's so funny?"

"Us, this. I'll be damned if we aren't perfect for each other."

"I love you, Tanner."

"Come here," Tanner said, and kissed her.

When the kiss ended, Sara stood and grabbed Alexa's clothing. "Do you think Alexa will want these things sent to her?"

"No, she said they were too worn to wear anymore."

"In that case, I'll toss them out."

"Along with our past?"

Sara pretended to hold a wine glass aloft. "To new beginnings."

7

TOO STUPID TO LIVE

Sammy was settled in a chair across from Joe's desk at the strip club, Johnny R's.

They were discussing Ricky Valente. Sammy had spent the last two days looking for Ricky and was certain that Ricky Valente had left the area.

"I talked to his girl, Seneca, the one that used to work at the old club. She said that she and Ricky broke up weeks ago."

"What's Seneca doing these days?"

"She owns a beauty parlor in Queens."

"Good for her, she's one of the smart ones who saved her money. Did she have any idea where we could find Ricky?"

"No, but she wasn't entirely surprised by Ricky's running off with the money. Seneca said he used to kid about it, but she never thought he was serious."

"Did you believe her, or is she maybe going to meet up with Ricky somewhere?"

Sammy waved that off. "I believed her. She and Ricky broke up because Ricky made a drunken pass at her little sister. She had no idea where Ricky went, but she said he might have gotten plastic surgery, you know, changed his face."

"Hmm, that will make him harder to find, but he can't go to a legitimate surgeon either, because he'd have to use his own name. Ricky will have to head underground for a cutter. I'll put out the word to our contacts in that world. There's only a handful of guys that do that sort of work."

"That's what I was thinking. Seneca also said that Ricky has a triangle-shaped burn mark."

"Where is the mark, on an arm?"

Sammy groaned. "The mark is on his damn butt, the left ass cheek. As you can guess, I'm hoping I won't need to look for it."

Joe laughed. "Maybe we'll find Ricky before he gets his face fixed."

"I want this one, Uncle Joe. I want to put Ricky down as a lesson to others. Stealing from us like that, the man is too stupid to live."

"He's all yours, but first, we have to find him."

IN NEW ORLEANS, RICKY VALENTE WAS LOOKING AT HIS face in a mirror and imagining it looking different. He didn't want to go overboard and have a whole new face, but make just enough changes to alter his appearance. He'd ask a surgeon to make his nose smaller, the lips fuller, and smooth the wrinkles around his eyes.

In the new life to come, Ricky wanted to look younger than his age, forty-one. He had already dyed his curly brown hair blond and had taken up running. Between the alterations to his face, the lighter hair, and a trimmer body, no one would recognize him when he came out into the open.

But that would wait, because the smart way to do things was to be patient. Other guys had stolen money from the mob over the years, and nine times out of ten they were tracked down and put down. Many of those failed attempts had ended when the thief contacted a plastic surgeon or an ID forger within days of running off.

That was too soon, much too soon, because it was the time when the people you'd stolen the money from were still fuming and eager to grab you. The word would go out that a reward was available. Anyone who resembled the thief would be eyed by the face doctors and the document forgers they were running to for help.

Six months. That was the way to go about it. Wait six months and then make your moves. The reward would be forgotten, the hot pursuit cooled down, and likely, there would be a new thief to chase after.

Despite popular belief, people steal from the various mobs all the time. Employee theft is always one of the biggest drains on a business's profit margin in the straight-laced world. It's no different in the crooked world.

But you had to be smart about it, and Ricky had thought things through. He had stolen a lot of money from the Giacconi Family, but it wasn't so much that Joe Pullo would be up nights worrying about it.

They'd look for him, oh yes they would, but in time, other problems would push the name Ricky Valente into the background. However, you had to be patient and you had to find a good place to wait things out.

Ricky was staying in a rented trailer. The trailer park itself was crowded with motor homes, but the section where Ricky was only had two old wrecks, and overgrown hedges blocked the view of them from the nearby highway.

The trailer park was owned by an old high school friend of Ricky's who had left New York decades ago. There was no way that anyone would connect the man to Ricky, who had paid the friend in cash to let him stay in the trailer. The friend was having financial problems due to a divorce. Ricky's money was welcomed like water in the desert, especially since it could be hidden from the tax man.

After paying off the plastic surgeon and arranging to buy a new ID in Florida, Ricky would still have nearly a quarter of a million left. That wasn't much in the states, but it would go a long way in parts of South America. Ricky wanted a new life and he had been bold enough to go for it.

A noise from outside made Ricky look away from the mirror. His neighbor was home. She was a young good-looking blonde who kept to herself as much as Ricky did. At first, Ricky had wondered if she were a hooker, but decided against it, since no one ever visited her. He had known more than a few hookers during his working years in the Giacconi Family, and his neighbor just didn't give off that vibe. Ricky had never talked to her, and knew he shouldn't talk to her, or anyone else. Still, maybe they'd hit it off, and she was damn good-looking.

The woman got out of the beater of a car she drove and gazed around warily. Ricky had seen her do that before, and figured she was just the jumpy type. He kept watching her, and this time he saw her do something new. She squinted at the door to her trailer, at a spot above the lock, then pulled a strand of hair away from that area. Ricky understood what she was doing. The woman had left a strand of her hair lodged in the door frame. If someone had entered her trailer during her absence, she'd know about it.

Satisfied that there were no intruders within, the woman went inside carrying a bag of groceries. After the door shut behind her, Ricky kept staring at it. His neighbor was more interesting than he realized, and maybe he wasn't the only one who was on the run.

RICKY VALENTE'S NEIGHBOR WAS A WOMAN NAMED JULIE Ryan. Julie was twenty-six and a former emergency room nurse from California. She was no longer a nurse because she'd been framed for stealing drugs from the hospital where she worked.

Drugs had gone missing, that was true, but Julie had no clue who had been taking them. The thefts stopped after an orderly had been killed in a mugging, and although no one wanted to speak ill of a dead colleague, the consensus of the staff was that the man had been the culprit. Then, the police showed up at the hospital with a warrant to search Julie's car, while other cops were searching her apartment. Drugs were discovered in both locations and Julie had been arrested and taken from the hospital in handcuffs. She refused any plea bargaining as she swore she was innocent. In time, she was schooled in the ways of the modern legal system by her lawyer.

"This is how it works, Julie," the lawyer said. "If you take the plea bargain you'll do six months in the county jail and then be set free. If you force the court to hold a trial for you, you'll do a year in county before you even see the inside of a courtroom."

"Why would I have to spend twice as long in jail?"

"Because the judge would think you're wasting her time. You know the evidence they have against you. The police found the drugs in your apartment, along with an envelope filled with money. A jury would find you guilty. If that happens, you'd be looking at ten years in prison. You're a young woman. Take the plea bargain, do the six months, and move on."

Reluctantly, Julie had taken the plea bargain, knowing that when she was released, she'd never work again as a nurse, a profession she loved.

Time inside the jail dragged while also being dangerous. Julie had been beaten twice by fellow inmates, although not badly. The family of doctors she came from all but disowned her, and while inside, her father passed away.

Finally, she was free and could start over, but she never felt safe. Someone had framed her for stealing drugs, and she still didn't know who had done it, or why they'd chosen her life to ruin. Julie was the recipient of at least one stroke of good luck when her father left her money in his will. It wasn't a fortune, but neither was it a pittance. The money would allow her the time she needed to decompress from her months spent in jail, before she had to reenter the workforce.

With no chance of going back into the work she was trained for, Julie decided to do what she thought she wouldn't get a chance to do until she had retired someday. She wanted to see the country from the road. She bought an old but mechanically sound car and headed out from California. She stayed along the coastline in the beginning. The trip was peaceful, regenerative, and she began to recover from her time in jail and the undeserved disgrace that had led her there. She had even stopped obsessing over whom it was that had framed her, as she motored along and put the past in the rearview mirror.

Then, Victor Fenner appeared. Fenner was in his

forties, wealthy, and came from a family that owned an insurance company. He was also insane.

Julie had been at a park in Oregon when Fenner approached her. For company while on the road, she had picked up a mutt from the pound. The dog was small, brown, and of indeterminate parentage. Julie loved the dog and named her Missy.

Missy growled at Fenner's approach, but that wasn't unusual, as Missy always growled at men and distrusted them.

Julie, being a good-looking woman, thought Fenner had settled beside her on the bench because he'd come over to make a pass at her. When the first words out of his mouth were a confession that he'd framed her, Julie stood and gawked down at him.

"What did you say?"

"I said, I'm the one who framed you for the theft of the narcotics. The reason I framed you, Julie, was to give you a glimpse of the power I have. I altered your life forever, and believe me when I tell you this, you now belong to me."

Tears sprang from Julie's eyes as anger welled up inside her. "Who are you?"

"My name doesn't matter, and soon, you'll be calling me Master."

Julie stared at the stranger in disbelief, and she saw the madness glittering in his eyes.

"Why would you do something like that to me? I don't even know you."

Fenner smiled. "I was always your destiny, and now, you'll belong to me forever."

Julie scooped up Missy in her arms and sprinted from the park. Her car was parked where she was staying, at a cheap motel only three blocks away. After gathering her belongings from the room, she was back on the road and fighting to hold the wheel steady.

Whoever that man was, if he was telling the truth it meant he was crazy. Julie had sometimes fantasized about clearing her name and being reinstated at the hospital. Having met her tormentor, she knew that would never happen.

It wasn't until she had stopped for the night at a motel in Washington State that she'd found the note from Fenner. It had been typed out in large bold letters. Julie had discovered it after flipping down her sun visor to check her face in the attached mirror.

YOU NOW BELONG TO ME, JULIE. SEE YOU SOON.

That was over a week ago. Julie had been on the run ever since.

8

WRONG PLACE, WRONG TIME

Alicino's Bakery on 28th Street was known for its apple turnovers. It was also a money drop for the Giacconi Family.

Over forty percent of the drug money collected each day in the city wound up in the basement of the bakery. Once there, the money was counted, banded, and packed in cake boxes. From there, the money was placed on a bakery truck that was armored and escorted by a group of six guards to a different location for money laundering.

The bakery had eight guards on duty inside the basement, while another four pretended to be bakers or customers. It was a real customer, an older woman in a faux fur coat, who first noticed that something was wrong.

While rubbing her eyes, she whispered, "Why am I so tired?" and then she collapsed to the floor. Before the guards could react, they too were overcome by the gas, as were the workers in the basement.

Three men entered the bakery wearing inconspicuous looking gas masks, while a fourth man, sans gas mask, stood outside the entrance munching on an apple turnover. There was a fifth man, their driver; he sat at the curb with the motor running. His partners were in the bakery for only eleven minutes and returned carrying five large garbage bags stuffed with cash.

The gas masks were removed, the men climbed into the car, and just as the driver was about to pull away from the curb, he heard someone call his name in a booming voice.

"Sean! Hey, Sean O'Doyle! How you doin' buddy?"

The driver stared at the man shouting his name as a curse escaped his lips. The man calling his name out in the street for anybody to hear was an old friend from the neighborhood he'd grown up in, back in Boston. The driver rolled his window down as the man came around to talk to him.

From the back seat, one of the men asked the driver a question. "You got this, or you want one of us to do it?"

"I got it," Sean said, even as he was taking out his gun.

The old friend from the neighborhood was named John Flynn. Flynn leaned his elbows on the window frame and smiled in at the group. "Hey guys, me and Sean here go way back."

"Yeah," Sean said. "About that, I'm sorry, Johnny. I really am."

Flynn looked confused. "You're sorry about what?"

"Wrong place, wrong time," Sean said, as he shot Flynn twice in the head. As the body was settling upon the street, Sean used his sleeve to wipe blood from his face. He then pulled away from the curb and headed back toward Boston.

∼

The following morning, Joe Pullo paced about his office at Johnny R's, which wouldn't be open for hours. With him were Sammy and Bosco. Bosco, Joe's right-hand man and Underboss of the Family, was confused by the way the robbery went down.

"That homemade knockout gas made sure they didn't have to kill anyone, so why shoot a civilian on the way out? I'm thinking there might be a connection between the thieves and the dead guy."

"We got a name on the dead guy yet?" Joe asked.

"Yeah, John Flynn."

"Flynn? That sounds Irish. Could he be from Boston?"

"I got one of our cops looking into it," Bosco said. "But Flynn had an apartment on Staten Island."

The phone on Joe's desk rang and he saw that the call was coming from downstairs in the club. He looked out of the one-way glass as he picked up the phone and saw an old woman standing in the doorway of the club with Tamir Ivanov, the club's manager.

"What's up, Fed?"

Ivanov stared up at the office as he spoke on the house phone the bouncers normally used. Although he only saw the club mirrored back at him, Ivanov guessed that Joe would be looking down at him.

"Joe, this woman is named Mrs. Carrera. She's asking to speak to you. She says it concerns the trouble at the bakery. Does that make sense to you?"

"Oh yeah, tell her I'll be right down."

Joe relayed Ivanov's call to Sammy and Bosco and the three of them took the elevator down to club level. Ivanov had the old woman settled at a table and one of the kitchen staff brought out a carafe of coffee.

"I'll be in the kitchen if you need me," Ivanov said.

Tamir Ivanov was in his forties, stood about six-feet tall and had ice-blue eyes. A former federal agent, Ivanov had aligned himself with the Giacconi Family after a cartel murder squad acting for the Russian mob killed his partner and lover, Justina Moretti.

Once they were alone at the table, with Sammy and Bosco watching from the bar, the old woman talked with Joe. She was white-haired and wizened, and when she spoke, her raspy voice betrayed her decades of cigarette smoking.

"Don Pullo, I have information about the trouble that went on at the bakery last night."

"Your name is Mrs. Carrera? Are you related to Carmine Carrera?"

"Yes, Don Pullo, Carmine was my son."

"He was a good man."

"He said the same about you, as do others."

"Tell me what you know."

Mrs. Carrera explained that she had been walking home from the store on the corner when she passed an alleyway beside the bakery and heard whispered voices. Just moments later, two men came out of the alley and walked toward the bakery's front door. They were joined by two more men, one of whom stayed out front while the other three put something on their faces and entered the bakery.

"I've been around a while now. I know trouble when I see it, so I ducked inside the doorway of a camera store and stayed in the shadows. When the men came out, that man who was killed called out to the driver of the car. He called the man Sean O'Doyle."

"You're certain of that name?"

Mrs. Carrera smiled as she tapped her forehead, then

her ears. "I forget things now and then, but there's nothing wrong with my hearing."

"Is there anything else you can tell me?"

"No, Don Pullo. I hope I have been helpful."

"You have been, Mrs. Carrera."

Joe called Bosco over. Bosco was a large man who was much smarter than his appearance would lead you to believe.

"Have Red drive Mrs. Carrera home in the limo."

"You got it, boss."

Joe smiled at the old woman. "I take it you live near the bakery. Do you like it there?"

"Oh yes, I raised Carmine in that apartment."

"As a show of gratitude, your rent will be taken care of."

The old woman lit up in a grin that displayed her tobacco-stained teeth. "You're paying my rent next month?"

"No, we'll be paying your rent forever. The information you gave us was valuable."

The old woman took Joe's hand and kissed it. "Bless you, Don Pullo. My Carmine was right about you."

Bosco had texted Red, the chauffeur, and told him to bring the limo around to the front of the club. Red came in through the front entrance and stood near Joe waiting for orders. Red's real name was Andre. He was only nineteen, had an average build, dark hair, and looked as naïve as he was.

"You'll be taking Mrs. Carrera home, Red, then come straight back here."

"Yes sir," Red said, before sending Mrs. Carrera a smile.

After Mrs. Carrera left, Joe filled Sammy and Bosco in on what the old woman had told him.

"It's sounding more and more like there's a Boston connection here," Bosco said.

Sammy nodded in agreement, but he pointed out something. "Even if a crew from Boston pulled the heist, I still think they needed inside information. Up until the point they killed Flynn, the operation was smooth as silk."

"You might be right, so we'll work that angle too, but I want to talk to this Sean O'Doyle."

"Should I have Rico and his crew make that happen?" Bosco asked.

"Or send me up there to Boston," Sammy said.

Joe shook his head. "If anyone from the Family handles this, there's a chance we could be going to war. I don't want to push that button yet, not until I know more."

"So what, we hire an outside crew?" Bosco asked.

"I'll ask Tanner to handle it, if he'll do it. It's not a hit, but it might need finesse."

"What about his busted wing," Bosco said.

"I talked to him yesterday and that splint is history. The arm is a little weak, but it works fine."

"All right then, I'll get our people on finding out if Moss Murphy even has a Sean O'Doyle working for him."

"Once you confirm it, I'll give Tanner a call."

Sammy tapped his fingers on the top of the table as he thought about the situation. When he stopped tapping, he asked Joe a question.

"Uncle Joe, you know Moss Murphy, is he crazy enough to think he can come in here and shove us out?"

"I wouldn't have thought so, but maybe when his son moved into Killburry without any trouble he decided to push his luck."

"We are taking back Killburry, yeah?"

"When the time is right, Sammy. There's just too damn much going on right now that I have no answers for."

"We know one thing for certain," Bosco said. "Someone is out to get us."

Joe barked out a laugh. "Everybody wants what they can't have."

9
WE MEET AT LAST

RICKY VALENTE STUDIED HIS FACE IN THE MIRROR AGAIN. It had become an obsession as he tried to imagine what he would look like after he had plastic surgery. Ricky always thought he was okay looking, but with a tweak here and there, he might be a handsome guy. The dyed blond hair already gave him a beach boy look, while the running regimen he'd begun, combined with a fat-free diet, and ban on beer, had taken twelve pounds off him.

Ricky stayed inside the trailer most of the time, but he had kept himself occupied by spying on his neighbor, Julie Ryan. Julie fascinated Ricky. The woman was either paranoid or on the run from someone.

Ricky had a New York Crime Family looking for him and he wasn't as cautious as Julie Ryan. Not only did the woman do the hair trick with the door every time she left her trailer, but for a while, she had worn a dark wig whenever she went out, as well as sunglasses and a floppy hat.

Late one night, when she thought no one was around to see, Ricky had watched Julie switch the license plates on her car. She had exchanged her California plates for a Louisiana license plate.

Ricky was sure of two things when it came to Julie Ryan. She was someone he'd like to spend time with, and the girl was running from somebody.

Ricky stepped out into daylight for the first time in weeks and felt the sun warm him. He'd been doing his running at night, partly to be less noticeable, but also because he was afraid and paranoid.

After weeks going by with nothing bad happening, he was feeling confident that no one would find him. Once he made his way down to Miami and got his new ID and face, Ricky Valente would cease to exist.

Ricky was stretching his muscles in preparation to run while thinking about what new name he would like to have, when Julie Ryan stepped out of her trailer with her dog. Ricky thought the dog was ugly, but he sure liked the look of its owner. He sent Julie a smile and said hello.

Julie pointed at his trailer. "Are you new here?"

"Um, yeah."

"I never saw the last person who rented that trailer, but I would see lights on at night and hear a TV playing."

Ricky had come up with a new name. He decided to try it out. "I'm Shane Ryder. It's nice to meet you."

Julie gave Ricky a tentative smile. "I'm Julie and this is Missy."

Ricky smiled at Missy and the dog growled at him.

"Were you taking the dog to the park?" Ricky asked.

"Why do you ask?"

"No biggie, but I was headed there. We could walk together and get to know each other, you know, like friendly neighbors."

Julie's smile was genuine this time. "Okay neighbor, but there's really not much to tell. I'm pretty boring."

"So am I," Ricky said. "So am I."

VICTOR FENNER, THE MAN WHO HAD FRAMED JULIE RYAN for drug theft, worked as an insurance investigator for a company owned by his family. Many people inside the insurance company thought it odd that Fenner would work in such a relatively low position, when he could easily be named a vice-president of a division.

When asked, the other members of the family pointed out Victor's record at catching insurance cheats, which was impressive. In truth, his family knew he was mentally unstable and let him do as he pleased. If Victor had wanted to be named the company's CEO, none of them would have stood in his way.

While Victor was still a teenager, his family had learned the folly of denying Victor what he wanted. One family member had paid with his life to learn that lesson.

As an insurance investigator for a top company, Victor was allowed access to any of the thousands of facilities his company insured. And he did the work, was good at it, and could spot a liar with ease. Victor never handled the simple cases, the ones where factory workers faked injuries to receive worker's compensation benefits, no, Victor liked a challenge.

He had stumbled upon the thieving orderly at Julie's hospital while working another case, and he had planned to hand the petty crook over to the police. But then, he saw Julie, and Victor knew he had to possess her.

She would be the fourth woman he possessed. The others were deceased, and it had been over three years since he'd found one he wanted to own.

He had demonstrated his power to Julie, had destroyed

her life to rebuild it to his liking. Were she to contact the authorities and tell them that he had admitted to framing her, they would not have listened.

Julie was an admitted thief. She had served time for those thefts after admitting her guilt in a plea bargain arrangement, and she was banned from ever working as a nurse again. On the other hand, Fenner came from a prestigious family and was good-looking enough to attract any number of women. He didn't need to go to extreme lengths to be with a woman.

Despite his history, there was no record of Victor Fenner ever being accused of stalking. That was because his technique was so unconventional. He never approached the women he desired until after he had ruined their reputations, and it was rare that he spoke to them at all in front of witnesses.

Fenner had no connection to Julie Ryan, and yet, he had altered her life forever. She had run away after their initial contact, and that was to be expected. She would need time to come to terms with her new reality. The fact was, Victor Fenner now owned her. If Julie Ryan ever hoped to have a moment of peace and a modicum of normalcy, she would have no choice but to give in to Fenner and become his lover.

Fenner returned to his hotel in Portland, Maine, after a day of watching the thief who had stolen artwork from the home of an insured client. He was certain the thief had stored the paintings in the home of the woman the thief was seeing, and convinced the woman had no idea.

Fenner sent off photos of the man entering and leaving the woman's basement by way of a window. The photos would wind up on the computer of the cop working the art theft, and the cop would owe Victor another favor.

At the hotel's front desk, Victor was told he had a

package. It was a FedEx envelope. After returning to his room, Victor opened the envelope and smiled. One of his contacts had come through for him.

Inside the envelope was a copy of the recent activity logged by Julie Ryan's electronic toll payments system. It told Fenner that she had traveled south and was now in New Orleans.

Fenner called the front desk, told them he would be checking out, and began packing. It was time to go to New Orleans.

10
BAD BOYS, BAD BOYS

Tanner and Sara entered a restaurant on East 7th Street in New York and found that Jake and Jennifer Garner were already seated at their table.

Tanner was dressed in a suit while Sara wore a dress. Jennifer and Jake were similarly attired and greeted them with subdued smiles.

Jake stood to pull out a seat for Sara, who sat to his left at the round table, while Tanner sat across from Jake and on Jennifer's right. When Jennifer reached over and placed her hand on of his for a moment, Tanner realized that she was trembling a bit.

"I want to thank you again for saving my life, Tanner."

"You're welcome, and I appreciate the invitation to have dinner with you. It means a lot to Sara."

Across the table, Jake Garner was laughing. When everyone looked at him, he gestured at Sara and Tanner,

"I'm sorry, it's just that, the two of you, together like this, well, it's one of the strangest sights I've ever seen. And yet, you do make a great-looking couple."

"If you'll recall, Jake, I wasn't happy when you and

Jennifer began dating. I was certain that you were just using her."

The waiter appeared and took Sara's and Tanner's drink orders, along with everyone's choice for a meal. After the drinks arrived, Jennifer looked at Jake with a conspiratorial smile.

"I'm going to tell Sara now."

"Tell me what?" Sara asked.

"I'm pregnant. I just found out today."

Sara leapt from her seat and moved around the table to hug her sister. As she did so, Tanner offered his congratulations to Jake, who looked to have mixed feelings about the news. Sara took note of Jake's solemnity and asked him about it.

"Jake, are you nervous about being a father for the first time?"

Jennifer looked uncomfortable and reached over to take her husband's hand.

"I was married once before, Sara," Jake said. "When I was much younger. My wife and I had two children. All three of them died in an accident."

Sara's hand flew to her mouth. "Oh no, I had no idea. Oh, Jake, I'm so sorry."

Jake shook his head. "I'm happy that Jennifer is pregnant, believe me I am. It's just that I…it's a little odd to think I'll be a father again."

"You feel guilty about having survived when your family died," Tanner said.

Jennifer looked shocked, not by the suggestion, but because Tanner had stated it. She had been thinking of him as a simple thug devoid of understanding.

Jake nodded. "Yes, I do feel guilt. I know I shouldn't, that I couldn't have changed anything by dying with them, but the guilt never goes away."

"It won't. You just have to live with it."

Jennifer was staring at Tanner as if he were a mannequin that had suddenly come to life. "Why do you know so much about this?"

Tanner sat motionless, then turned his head to look at Sara.

"You don't need to say anything," Sara told him.

After releasing a sigh, Tanner spoke. "My family was murdered when I was sixteen, even my baby brother and younger sisters. Only I survived."

Jennifer fell back in her seat as she whispered, "Good Lord."

The table grew quiet, and before anyone spoke again, the food came. After the waiter left them with the promise of bringing fresh drinks, Sara looked around the table.

"So much for casual dinner conversation, hmm?"

Jennifer smiled. "I wanted to get to know more about Tanner tonight, and I've certainly done that. He's not the typical bad boy that I thought he was."

"Bad boy?" Tanner said.

Jennifer pointed at Sara. "My sister has always liked bad boys, including Johnny Rossetti, and now yourself."

"I don't like boring men," Sara said. "And Tanner is anything but boring."

WHEN DINNER WAS OVER, THEY MOVED TO THE BAR FOR coffee. Sara and Jennifer sat together, while Jake spoke with Tanner.

"It's a funny thing how there's no record of you in the databases anymore, Tanner. How did you manage that?"

"What do you mean?"

"Those mugshots the Mexican authorities took of you

are gone from all official databases, along with the records of your fingerprints. You didn't know?"

Tanner wore a small smile. "No, but I think I can thank a man named Lawson for that."

"Thomas Lawson?"

"You know him?"

"Not personally, but yeah, he has that much clout."

"So I've noticed."

To Tanner's left, Jennifer was passing along a telephone number to Sara.

"Alicia Kincaid," Sara said. "I haven't talked to her in years. How is she?"

"Great, she owns a dance studio in The Village. She said that there was something she wanted to speak to you about."

"I wonder what that could be. Anyway, it will be good to see her again, I miss her."

"She still resembles you so much. Remember when all the teachers thought you two were sisters?"

"Some even thought we were twins, but by the time we reached high school I was several inches taller than her."

"Anyway, give her a call, and Sara?"

"Yeah?"

"I hope things work out for you and Tanner. If he makes you happy, that's good enough for me."

"Thanks, now, how far along are you?"

"Only a few weeks, and I can't wait to find out the baby's sex."

"Do you want a boy or a girl?"

"I don't really have a preference; I just hate not knowing."

"A good friend of Tanner's had a daughter, and someone else we know is pregnant, and now you."

"What about you? Is that something you would want?"

Sara nodded. "I definitely want to be a mother someday."

"How would Tanner feel about that?"

Sara's grin was wide. "He'd love it, although I doubt he knows that yet."

Jennifer looked past Sara's shoulder, to where Tanner sat talking with Jake.

"Tanner is deeper than I would have thought."

"There's a heart there too, and a good sense of humor."

"I remember when you thought he was nothing more than a killing machine," Jennifer said.

Sara smiled in return. That was one opinion of hers about Tanner that hadn't changed. The man was a killing machine, and the deadliest man alive.

11
BEANTOWN

Bosco confirmed that Moss Murphy had a Sean O'Doyle in his organization and Joe asked Tanner if he'd be willing to grab O'Doyle and bring him back to New York City. The request came as they were at a midtown gun club and practicing their shooting. Sammy was with them, but he had stepped out to take a call.

"I know it's not your usual thing, Tanner, but I can count on you not to screw it up and I don't want our fingerprints on this."

"Aren't you afraid I might kill him out of habit?"

"No, but on the other hand, I don't necessarily need him in one piece."

Tanner's left arm still had some residual weakness from the injury he'd suffered in Siberia. He worked it hard by shooting rifles until he found it difficult to raise the weapon.

"How's that arm?" Joe asked.

"It's coming along."

"I want O'Doyle alive, but if you have to ice him, ice

him. Anyway, the word is the guy hangs out with his crew, so you'll have to wait until he's alone."

"That's easy. I'll take him in his apartment."

Sammy returned from taking his call and held up the phone. "Good news. Some ex-hooker down in New Orleans has ratted Ricky out for the reward."

"Are you sure it's him?"

"Yeah, the old lady took a picture of him in a park. He's dyed his hair blond, but it's him. Why don't I fly down there tonight?"

Joe thought that over, then shook his head. "Ricky will wait a day or two. I want you with me until we hear what O'Doyle has to say."

Sammy scowled with disappointment. "I don't want Ricky to crawl into a hole somewhere."

"One more day, or we could farm it out?"

"No, that bastard is mine. I'll wait."

They left the gun club and Tanner saw Joe's chauffeur, Red, talking to a beautiful girl with long dark hair. Red was smiling a silly grin. When the girl spotted Joe, she waved.

"Tanner," Joe said. "That's Johnny Rossetti's little sister, Gina."

"I see the resemblance, and she's not so little."

"Yeah, she's a looker."

Gina walked over smiling, as her eyes wandered over Tanner.

"Hi Joe, I was driving by and saw the limo, so I thought I'd stop and say hi."

"I'm glad you did, and meet a friend of mine. His name is Tanner."

Gina's smile faltered just a bit when she heard Tanner's name and Tanner wondered why. Perhaps she had heard that he'd been there when her brother was killed.

"It's a pleasure to meet you, Mr. Tanner. But Joe, I

know you're busy, and I have things to do too. I just didn't want to miss a chance to see you."

"Be sure to let me know if you need anything, Gina, and I mean anything. Johnny would want me to look out for you."

"That's sweet, Joe, but all's right with my world. See you around."

"What did she study in college?" Tanner asked.

"Chemistry, or something brainy like that."

"Hmm, so she's good-looking and smart, just like her brother. Now about Boston, when would you like me to go?"

"Tonight, buddy, and thanks."

Two nights after having dinner with Jennifer and Jake, Tanner was in Boston, inside the apartment of Sean O'Doyle. He'd been waiting for O'Doyle to arrive home for over two hours. During that time, he had given the apartment a gentle search, making certain that he put everything back where it belonged. After finding a thick envelope stuffed with cash taped to the back of a table in the bedroom, Tanner kept it to give to Joe. The money was possibly from the robbery of the bakery anyway.

With his gun in hand, Tanner crouched behind a chair that sat in a corner of the living room, as O'Doyle was opening his front door. He almost revealed himself, but he froze when he heard voices.

O'Doyle wasn't alone. There was a man with him who had an Irish accent. The two of them talked while standing in the open doorway. Tanner couldn't get a look at the guy, knowing that if he were to lift his head up above the chair he'd be spotted.

"I still don't know why you're here to see me," O'Doyle said.

"You seem nervous to me, Sean. Are you nervous?"

"No, I'm tough and smart. Are you here to deliver a message?"

"If I was here to deliver a message, the type you mean, you would already have received it loud and clear."

O'Doyle sighed. "Are you ever gonna tell me why you were parked outside my building, or do you want me to guess?"

"There's a rumor going around that the Giacconis got one of their cash drops hit. Do you know anything about that?"

"No."

"No?"

"No, I don't know anything, and I wouldn't make a move like that without Moss's say-so."

"Where were you three nights ago?"

"Gee, Officer, let me try to remember."

"Don't get cute, just answer the question."

"Ah, me and my boys were hangin' here."

"You sure?"

"Yeah, I remember now. We watched the Celtics game."

"Who won the game?"

"I did. I bet against the Celtics. They ain't been right since Larry Bird retired."

There were a few moments of silence before the Irishman spoke again.

"Keep an ear to the ground. If you hear anything, tell me or Moss."

"Sure," O'Doyle said. That was followed by the sound of the door closing.

Tanner was again delayed from revealing himself when O'Doyle plopped down in the chair he was crouched behind. By the sound of things, O'Doyle was making a phone call to someone. It was probably to the other members involved in the heist, to make certain they had their stories straight.

A voice answered, but the sound was too faint for Tanner to make out.

As expected, O'Doyle was calling to warn one of the other members of the heist crew. Tanner was sick of being behind the damn chair. He stood, reared back a fist, and delivered a solid blow to O'Doyle's right temple.

Sean O'Doyle went tumbling from the chair and Tanner walked around from behind it and kicked the other side of O'Doyle's head. O'Doyle was out cold, but the phone he dropped was emitting a tinny voice. By the time Tanner picked it up and placed it to his ear, the line was dead.

Tanner bound O'Doyle's wrists behind his back, blindfolded him, then stuffed and secured a gag in the punk's mouth. It took over ten minutes for O'Doyle to regain his senses. When he came to, he began to panic. Tanner had made it impossible for Sean O'Doyle to see or speak, but he could still hear and feel. He froze when he felt the barrel of the gun beneath his chin, which was accompanied by Tanner's voice.

"I won't kill you if you do what I say. We're going to walk out of here with me guiding you by the arm, understand? If you understand, nod."

After a hesitation, O'Doyle nodded.

"Fine, now let's go."

O'Doyle was wearing a hoodie. Tanner yanked the hood up, then pulled the top of it forward, to obscure the blindfold.

"Keep your head down. Don't try anything stupid or I'll knock you out again and carry you."

O'Doyle mumbled a reply and Tanner told him to shut up. They rode down to the parking garage in the elevator without seeing anyone, although there was a couple on the other side of the garage talking about a movie they had just seen.

Pullo had supplied Tanner with a white van that had Massachusetts license plates. Before the thug knew what was happening, Tanner bound O'Doyle's ankles and shoved him into the rear of the van.

The van had tinted windows, and its metal walls were lined with plywood that was covered by the type of thick pads used by movers to protect furniture. O'Doyle could kick at the van's walls to attract attention, but the sound would be muffled. The floor was covered in plywood as well, with an old mattress for O'Doyle to lie on.

Tanner drove out of the garage. While stopped at a nearby light, Tanner saw a car brake to a hard stop in front of O'Doyle's building. Afterward, a young man with red hair got out of the car and ran inside.

It was probably the person O'Doyle had been talking to on the phone, coming to see what ill had befallen Sean.

Tanner drove back toward New York City without incident, other than the occasional muffled sounds coming from the rear of the van.

All in all, it had been a quiet night.

Too bad it wouldn't last.

Later, back in New York City, Johnny R's was closing for the night and the dancers were going home. As two of them walked past the bar, a blonde and a brunette, they smiled at Red, the chauffeur, as they told him goodnight.

Red smiled back, without making eye contact, and one of them, the blonde, pinched him on the cheek.

"You are going to be so cute when you grow up."

"I'm already grown," Red said, "and I got a girl too."

The brunette pretended to pout, then spoke to her friend. "We missed our chance, April."

Behind the bar, Tamir Ivanov was watching the dancers tease Red. "That's enough, ladies, and have a good night."

The blonde stuck her tongue out at Ivanov. "We're just playing, but I meant it, he is cute. Bye-bye, Red."

Red watched them go and Ivanov came around the bar to sit beside him. The former FBI man had taken a liking to Red, and as they were both of Russian extraction, he felt a kinship with the boy as well.

"Do you really have a girl, Andre, and how come I've never met her?"

Red smiled, leaned in, and whispered. "It's Gina Rossetti."

A look of surprise showed on Ivanov's face. "Really, how long has that been going on?"

"A few weeks, but she wants to keep it a secret, so don't say anything, okay?"

"I won't, but why keep it a secret?"

"She thinks Mr. Pullo wouldn't approve of our dating, you know, because I'm just a chauffeur."

"I know Joe is like an uncle to the girl, but I don't think he would try to keep you away from Gina. Anyway, congratulations, that is one beautiful girl. Are you two getting serious?"

Red shrugged. "We've kissed, but you know, that's it so far."

Ivanov smiled. "It sounds like you might have yourself an old-fashioned girl there."

∼

IN NEW ORLEANS, RICKY VALENTE SAT IN A FOLDING chair at the rear of his rented trailer and looked across at Julie Ryan. She had stopped wearing the brown wig and dark glasses, but Ricky knew she still placed a hair in the door frame before leaving her trailer.

After their first meeting, Ricky had made it a point to be in the park at the same time as Julie, as he tried his best to get her to like him. Her dog, Missy, didn't like Ricky, that was plain to see. The hound growled at him whenever he tried to pet her. Julie told him not to take offense. Missy had been abused as a puppy and didn't seem to like anyone but Julie.

For her part, Julie enjoyed Ricky's company. She had been lonely, and although Ricky wasn't her type, and she would never think of him as more than a friend, he did ease her loneliness. She had to fend off his advances, while reminding him that she wasn't looking to get involved with anyone. So far, Ricky had backed-off. If not for the loneliness, Julie would have kept her distance from him.

However, she hadn't been with anyone she could just sit and talk with since before going to prison. Talking with Ricky made her forget what a mess her life was. The two shared a love of old movies and had similar taste in music as well. Over a six-pack of beer, which Ricky had drunk most of, they had sat and talked for hours.

When they ran out of small talk, Ricky asked a question he'd been dying to ask.

"Hey Julie, who are you running from, honey?"

"What?"

"I can tell you're on the run from somebody. If it's the law, that's cool, but if it's a guy, I can help you."

"Help me, how?"

"So, it is a guy?"

Julie stood, as her eyes began to tear up. "I don't want to talk about it."

She started toward her trailer and surprised an old woman who had been skulking near the side of Ricky's RV. It was the old woman who had told the Giacconi Family where to find Ricky. Years earlier, a much younger Ricky had broken the arm of a friend of hers over a late payment.

The ex-hooker had remembered Ricky's face when she saw him, despite the dyed blond hair. When she spoke to the friend in New York, she learned that Ricky was wanted by the Giacconis for stealing from them.

The old woman laid a hand on her chest and sighed at Julie. Because of the late hour, the woman was dressed in her robe and slippers. "You scared me."

"What are you doing over here?" Ricky asked her.

"I… you need to be quiet. People are trying to sleep."

"Were we loud?" Julie said. "If so, I apologize."

"All right then, and ah, goodnight."

As the woman walked off, Ricky spoke under his breath. "What an old bat."

Julie crossed her arms over her chest. "How would you help me?"

"I'm good with my fists, but I know how to use a gun too."

Julie wiped at tears. "I don't want him dead. I just want him to leave me alone."

"Who is he, an ex-husband?"

"No," Julie said. "He's a madman."

By 2:28 A.M., Tanner was thirty minutes away from Johnny R's and driving along a stretch of highway that had its inner lane under construction. Concrete barriers and orange cones directed the traffic into the outer lanes.

During the morning rush hour, the delay turned the highway into a parking lot, but it made no difference because of the late hour. The nearest car in front of Tanner was thirty car lengths ahead. There were two sets of headlights moving up close behind him, and it was their speed that alerted Tanner that there might be trouble brewing.

If not for his training and experience, his attention would have stayed focused on the vehicles coming up from behind. Instead, Tanner took a moment to survey his surroundings. He spotted three men dressed in black who were climbing down from a huge yellow dump truck they had just used to block the road a half mile ahead.

The men then crossed onto the other side of the concrete dividers, where they were steadying their rifles, while waiting for their target to draw closer. The rifles were full-auto Romanian AK-47's with hundred-round drums attached. Although they'd be aiming at a moving target, they were certain to hit the van with dozens of rounds.

Traveling between the set of concrete construction barriers, Tanner could neither turn right nor left. He was in a tunnel, with two vehicles at the rear, a massive truck blocking the exit and a virtual firing squad ready to slice him into little pieces.

So much for a quiet night.

12
FIRST CONTACT

Ricky had convinced Julie to come inside his trailer to talk, and they did so, while drinking more beer.

Julie told Ricky about her past, and how she had been framed and served time. Ricky then surprised himself by opening up in return. He didn't explain why or tell Julie his real name, but he confessed to her that he was on the run as well.

"This guy, Julie, the nut that framed you, you really don't know his name?"

"Shane, I never saw him before, and there he was just calmly telling me how he ruined my life. I truly believe he must be insane."

"If he shows up here, I'll plant him in a shallow grave."

"Don't even joke. I hope I never see him again," Julie said.

She stifled a yawn, looked at her watch, and was shocked at how late it was. "Wow, we've been talking a long time, and I have to get up early."

"Why, you don't have anywhere to be, do you?"

Julie smiled. "I volunteered to work at a homeless shelter, and I start tomorrow."

"What's it pay?"

Julie laughed. "It pays nothing. I'm volunteering, remember? But I will get a free meal that will help me stretch my money."

"Back in New York City, some of those volunteers at the UN pull in good dough, thousands a month is what I hear. There are other volunteer jobs like that too. They call it a 'stipend', but I say money is money."

"I've never been to New York City. Did you live there for long?"

"Born and raised."

Julie stifled another yawn. As she walked by Ricky to return to her trailer, he reached out and took her hand.

"You could stay here tonight."

Julie sighed. "Shane…I—"

Ricky released her. "You can't blame me for trying, Julie, and someday you'll give in."

"Goodnight, Shane."

"It could have been," Ricky mumbled.

Julie laughed, leaned over, and pecked Ricky on the cheek. "See you tomorrow, and stop drinking so much beer. I thought you were on a diet?"

"Oh, right, but man I love beer."

Moments later, Julie and her dog, Missy, disappeared into her trailer.

Less than a hundred feet away, in the shadows, Victor Fenner watched and waited.

TANNER RELEASED THE STEERING WHEEL AND DIVED INTO the rear of the van. He landed on the mattress, facing the gagged and blindfolded Sean O'Doyle. Tanner gripped O'Doyle by his belt and wiggled against the passenger side of the van. That was where the sliding side door was, and where the floor of the van was lower and contained a built-in step.

Without a steady hand at the wheel, the van veered to the left and bounced off one of the concrete dividers. The impact sent it to the right, where it hit a divider on that side. The effect made the van slow sooner than it would have, something Tanner was counting on.

Tanner held on tightly to O'Doyle's form, as he lowered the left side of his own body down onto the metal step by the side door. That left O'Doyle in front of, and slightly over him to act as a human shield. Once the shooting began, O'Doyle took multiple rounds, while bits of glass from the windows filled the air and the tires went flat from bullet holes.

Although they wouldn't stop a round on their own, Tanner was grateful for the sheets of plywood lining the van's walls. The bullets had to penetrate the vehicle's thin steel walls, the plywood, the furniture pads, then the body of Sean O'Doyle. Every bit of it helped to sap energy from the rounds and kept them from exiting O'Doyle and hitting Tanner.

The van came to a jarring stop as it reached the dump truck. The vehicle rebounded away, but was halted by one of the dividers, then it drifted back toward the dump truck again. Before the van came to rest, Tanner had opened the side door and jumped out as far as his legs would take him.

He vaulted over the barrier to land on his hands and feet, before sprinting for the trees in a zigzag pattern. Tanner, dressed in black, was a dark shape among the shadows of the night and had gone unseen by his attackers.

After Tanner's departure, the van had bumped against the dump truck once more and the impact caused the bloody body of Sean O'Doyle to slide halfway out the side door. Meanwhile, the gunfire continued. The shooters had discarded the spent 100-round drums and reloaded with standard 30-round magazines. Despite the lack of return fire, they sent more rounds into the van.

While that was happening, the cars at the rear had parked, and a man got out of each vehicle. One of them was the mastermind of the hit on Tanner. His name was Esau Ramirez.

Esau grinned and slapped the man with him on the back as they moved closer to the van and saw what hundreds of rounds of ammo could do. No one could have survived that barrage, not even the man who called himself Tanner.

Esau was a thug and a member of a street gang, but he was an intelligent thug who was well-read and prided himself on his knowledge of military tactics. He had studied the battles of Napoleon and Alexander the Great. He had also devoured the works of Carl von Clausewitz and Sun Tzu.

Having advanced knowledge of where Tanner had been headed and what he would be driving was all the advantage Esau had needed. He used several vehicles to follow Tanner so that he would never pick up the tail.

They had lost sight of him only for a short time, when Tanner had driven the van into an underground parking garage in Boston. Even that was good, as it gave Esau time to work out where the hit should take place. It had to take place in New York, Not anywhere in Massachusetts, and certainly not inside the city of Boston, or it could be tied to the Irish mob. When Tanner left the garage and headed back toward New York City, the hit was in play, and it had gone down perfectly.

Esau's grin expanded as he saw the legs sticking out of side door of the van. Three of his men, the ones who had done the shooting, were firing shots in the air. They had to keep the traffic from coming closer, while dissuading the cars on the other side of the highway from rubbernecking. That meant that dozens of calls were being made to the police, but Esau still had to verify his kill.

The three men who were firing joined Esau just as he and the driver of the other car reached the van.

Esau's smile disappeared when he saw that the corpse's wrists were bound behind its back. There had been a blindfold, but one of the shots that passed through the metal body of the van had removed it as the round had exited out of O'Doyle's left eye socket.

"That ain't Tanner," one of the shooters said, then all five men began searching the shadows with their eyes.

Esau cursed, knowing he had lost the battle and needed to regroup. They had left a vehicle parked up the road, it was a huge black pickup truck they would use to flee the scene. It was tucked away off the road, between more of the concrete barriers.

Esau and his men ran around the dump truck with their guns at the ready. Tanner was out there somewhere, likely hidden among the sparse trees where the light from the highway couldn't reach.

Esau cursed his luck and damned his negligence. While it was true that Tanner had been fortunate to have a sacrificial lamb to shield him from the bullets, it was also true that Esau should have brought along men and hidden them in the trees.

If he had caught Tanner in a crossfire, the man would be dead. After jogging past the dump truck, Esau and his men made a beeline for the pickup they would escape in. It never occurred to Esau that, like Tanner had been, he and his men were penned-in between two concrete barriers.

They had left the truck running to make a hasty escape, so no one thought anything about the sound of the engine until it revved up. When the white reverse lights blazed to brilliance it was too late to react in time to escape, and the four-ton truck was rocketing backwards toward them.

INSIDE THE TRUCK, TANNER KEPT HIS FOOT ON THE GAS. He ran over the first three men and the truck jounced over their bodies, then the fourth man went airborne, to land on his skull, which shattered, spilling his brains on the highway.

Tanner only stopped the truck after he smeared Esau against one of the concrete barriers. He exited the vehicle to the sound of approaching sirens. But before Tanner ran off into the trees, he and the dying Esau locked eyes.

ESAU HAD JUST ENOUGH TIME TO REGISTER THE TRUCK coming at him before hearing the screams of his men. A second and a half later, he was letting out a scream of his own as his legs were crushed and his torso was mangled. He couldn't breathe after that, and the pain that had been so intense an instant earlier was fading away. Looking up past the bumper of the truck that had him pinned, Esau watched as Tanner emerged from the vehicle. It struck him how average the man looked, that is, until he saw Tanner's eyes.

The man had the most intense gaze he had ever seen. Then, Tanner was staring at him, or rather, at his tattoos, the ones on his face. Tanner used the light from his phone to view the tattoos of Esau's crew, or rather, what was left of them, then he leapt over a barrier with a graceful move, to sprint away.

Esau, who was also a fan of Shakespeare, was shuffling off his mortal coil. However, it wasn't a quote from the Bard of Avon that passed through Esau's mind in the final moments of his life. Rather, it was a quote from a famous military strategist, Field Marshal Helmuth von Moltke.

Von Moltke, once said that, "No battle plan survives contact with the enemy."

That quote was never truer than when Tanner was the enemy.

Esau died on the highway like roadkill, just another in a long line of men who had underestimated Tanner.

13

LAUNDRY DAY

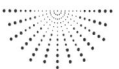

Tanner left the chaos on the highway behind him as he bolted into the trees. There weren't many of them, just a strip of land, beyond which lay a city street. He knew he was in Upper Manhattan but wasn't certain what section.

The sound of sirens was growing louder and seemed to be coming from several directions. There were six dead men lying back on the highway. The cops would go all out to catch the man who killed them. Tanner had no fear of leaving prints behind, as he had worn gloves, but he knew his image must have been captured on numerous traffic cameras. That was all right as well, because the cap he'd been wearing had a long bill in front that would have obscured most of his face from overhead cameras.

While he hadn't gone to Boston on a hit, he had still been there to commit a crime. He was dressed in black from head to toe and looked like a second-story man. Any cop crossing his path would detain him, and once they found the lock picks he carried, or his gun, he'd wind up in a jail cell.

Of course, he hadn't killed O'Doyle, but he had

abducted him and killed five others. Also, O'Doyle's splattered blood was on his clothing.

Tanner ran through city streets in the early morning hours that was home to sparse traffic and vacant of pedestrians. The terrain was hilly, and so he reasoned he was in the Hudson Heights section of Manhattan, where the land sat high above sea level.

After catching a glimpse of the George Washington Bridge between buildings, Tanner dropped to the ground behind a parked vehicle as a patrol car cruised down the street. After the car passed, he looked in the direction it had come from and saw a lit storefront several blocks away.

Tanner moved in that direction, as his mind raced to formulate a plan. As he drew closer to the store with the lit windows, he passed a donut shop. It was one of the chain stores. When he spotted the bin in the rear parking lot, he headed for it. It was a receptacle that accepted clothes for donations. Tanner picked the cheap lock with ease and found a set of worn jeans and a shirt that would fit him, along with a baseball jacket that had a bleach stain on its back. As he looked around, he caught a better view of the store that was open. It wasn't a store after all, but an all-night laundromat.

A plan bloomed in Tanner's mind. He scooped up more clothes, relocked the bin, and moved behind it to change out of sight. He had done so just in time, as a police car came around the corner of the building and shone a spotlight around. Seeing nothing amiss, the car moved on, but as he was dressing, Tanner spotted the search light of another patrol car as it came down the street he'd been walking on.

He had to get to that laundromat, and he had to do it soon, but first, he needed one more thing. There was an apartment house on the next corner. Tanner found the front door unlocked, but he had to pick the lock on an inner door.

Once inside, he considered changing his plan and finding an apartment to hide in. Although, after more consideration, that seemed a bigger gamble than his first plan, as it would risk involving hostages and any number of unpredictable variables, such as unknowingly entering the apartment of a cop.

Deciding to stick with his first idea, Tanner moved toward the mailboxes on the left. There were only twelve apartments in the building, but he needed a name that might fit him. A narrow table sat before the mailboxes with a trashcan beneath it.

There was a full-length mirror on the wall beside the door that sat next to a dented umbrella stand. Tanner used a penlight to check his hands for signs of blood, then did the same for his face in the mirror. He was clean of dried blood.

He sent a quick text off to a phone that Joe Pullo would know to check for messages.

THE PACKAGE WAS DESTROYED, BUT THE COURIER IS FINE. MORE LATER.

A look inside the trashcan revealed a lot of old mail that had been thrown out. There was plenty of it, primarily junk mail and advertisements. However, one envelope held a letter from a bank detailing the late charges on a checking account. The letter was addressed to Daniel Swyers.

Tanner searched the mailboxes. After he found one with the name D. SWYERS taped onto it, he stuffed the letter from the bank into the pocket of the bleach-stained jacket he'd taken from the donation bin.

He then broke into Swyers' mailbox and found it empty. He crammed his gun, spare ammo, phone, and lock pick set into the mailbox. He also squeezed the envelope of cash found in Sean O'Doyle's apartment inside the box. He hadn't needed the lock picks to get past the tiny lock on the mailbox, a hard tug was all it took. The box locked again once a hard shove was applied, and Tanner was ready.

Someone had donated clothes by placing them inside a cloth laundry bag with a tear on its side. Tanner walked into the laundromat with that same bag full of worn clothes and waved and said hello to the old woman sitting behind a scarred wooden counter. She was Asian. Her hair was streaked with white and she was smoking a cigarette.

After getting change from the old woman, Tanner loaded the hand-me-down clothes into a washing machine. With the machine running, he turned to see a cop car moving along slow on the street outside.

Tanner sat in one of the cheap plastic chairs, picked up an automotive magazine that was a year old, crossed his legs at the ankles, and pretended to read. He also used his fingers to comb his hair forward. He was aware that his eyes were intense, and the unkempt hair would help to distract from them. Besides, it was the middle of the night. Who worries about how their hair looks in a laundromat at three a.m.?

They came inside four minutes later. Two male cops in their thirties with eyes that searched every corner. As one of the cops, a black man, kept an eye on him, his white partner went toward the rear and spoke to the old woman.

Tanner looked up from his magazine and pretended to appear dismayed by the attention the cops were giving him. "Is something wrong?" he asked the cop standing near him.

"Kinda late to be doing laundry, isn't it?"

Tanner shrugged. "I have insomnia, so I figured why not at least get something done."

Two more cops entered, and this time they were young, no more than twenty-five. One was a white male who swaggered as he walked, while the Hispanic female had short hair and a pretty, but no-nonsense face. The two of them whispered something to the other cop, then all three proceeded to stare at Tanner. When the cop who had been talking to the old woman joined them, he shared some news.

"The woman back there says he just walked in a few minutes before we arrived, but that he did have a bag of laundry."

"Did she say he was a regular?"

"No, she's never seen him before."

"What's going on?" Tanner asked, and was ignored, as he expected he would be. Cops asked questions, they rarely answered them.

The cop who had spoken to the old lady talked in a low tone to his partner. Whatever he said made the partner head back to the patrol car. As the two young cops stood by and stared at him, the other cop spoke to him.

"Seems a little late to be doing laundry."

"Yeah, but like I told the other officer, I have insomnia."

"Is that right?"

"Unfortunately, yes."

The cop said nothing more, but he gestured for the two young cops to join him outside, where they stood blocking the door. Tanner figured if he were to run for a rear exit, he might make it outside, but then what? There were cops on the prowl everywhere. He just needed to let his plan work itself out.

After a couple of minutes, Tanner stood. The younger

cops went on alert like two English Pointers after a pheasant, but relaxed when Tanner grabbed a coffee from a vending machine and sat back down. As he was walking back toward them, one of the older cops, the black one, was looking back and forth between the computer tablet he was holding and Tanner's face.

Tanner understood what the cop was doing. He was comparing video from a tollbooth or traffic camera with his face. He remained calm because he was certain they had no good photos of him. At best, they had pictures of his chin and mouth. They were waiting for something, possibly more evidence, a witness, or just hassling him until they found another suspect, but for now, he was their man.

Ten more minutes ticked by slowly, but Tanner remained calm. Worry would accomplish nothing, and things would go the way things would go. Either his ruse would work, or he'd be arrested and held on suspicion. He thought his odds were good, so he sat and sipped on his coffee. The coffee was decaf, such as an insomniac would drink. Every so often, he would turn his head and glance at the cops with a look of confusion displayed on his face. Meanwhile, the cops stared back at him with deadpan expressions.

A third police car appeared. It was an SUV and had the word SUPERVISOR written on it in bold green lettering. An older man came out of the car. He was white and weighed as much as the two young cops combined. He spoke to his people, then listened while staring through the window at Tanner. With a nod and a smug look, he waddled inside the laundromat and toddled over to stand before Tanner.

"You, get on your feet."

Tanner did as ordered, then the older cop spoke again.

"What's your name?"

Tanner answered while stuttering a bit. He wasn't nervous about the five cops glaring at him, but he knew that most people would be, so he played the role.

"Da…Daniel, I'm Daniel Swyers."

"Swyers, hmm? Let's see some ID."

Tanner reached around to his back pocket and the young male cop's hand settled on the butt of his gun.

"Ah crap, I think I left my wallet at home."

The fat cop was smiling, and he sent knowing looks to the two older patrolmen.

"You just happened to leave your wallet home… how convenient."

"Wait, let me check my jacket pockets."

They waited, and when Tanner's hand came out of the right-side pocket, he was holding the letter from the bank he'd salvaged from the garbage. Rather than bring it to their attention, Tanner tossed it into the trashcan that was positioned near the chairs. It was a gamble to discard it, but it would look like the prop it was if he made a show of handing it over himself.

"Yeah, I guess I left my wallet home. But I live right up the street there at that apartment house."

The young female cop reached into the trashcan and took out the envelope. Tanner could have kissed her.

After reading the envelope and its contents, surprise lit the cop's pretty face, then she passed the envelope along to the fat cop. "Lieutenant, sir, look at this."

The fat cop pulled his gaze away from Tanner to look first at the female cop, then at what she was holding in her hand. "What is it?"

"It's the envelope he tossed in the trash. His name is on it, along with an address that's right up the block."

"What?"

The lieutenant scanned the envelope's contents. As he

did so, his shoulders slumped, and a small sigh escaped him. He stared at Tanner once more as if making up his mind about something, and a buzzer sounded, indicating that the wash cycle was completed.

Tanner looked around at the cops before gesturing at the washer. "Is it all right if I keep doing my clothes?"

The fat cop ignored him and barked new orders to the others. It seemed as if they were going to look elsewhere for their suspect.

Tanner continued to play his part and moved the clothes into the dryer. When he looked up, the last of the cop cars was leaving the parking lot. He sat down in his seat and went back to looking through the car magazine. Once the clothes were done, he walked back to the apartment house and dropped the laundry bag on the floor, near the mailboxes.

Tanner watched from the foyer of the building, but he saw only one police car go by in the next hour. They would come to believe that their suspect had escaped, and the roadblocks would end. The coffee shop where Tanner stole the clothes out of the bin opened for business before dawn. Tanner reclaimed his belongings from the mailbox and walked down for a breakfast of coffee and a whole-wheat donut.

He'd told Sara that he wouldn't make it back to her apartment in Connecticut before morning and knew that she'd be asleep. Still, he sent her a text saying that he was all right, then added that he'd like to meet her in the city.

Once that was done, he texted Joe Pullo again, then sipped on another cup of coffee. About an hour later, Sammy Giacconi pulled up in a black BMW. Tanner settled beside him in the passenger seat and studied Sammy. The kid had changed, as Joe had told Tanner. The old Sammy had a playful nature and a ready smile. The man seated beside Tanner looked neither playful nor cheerful. He was a serious person with responsibilities and a heart broken by grief.

Sammy voiced his own observation about Tanner's appearance. Tanner was still wearing the worn jeans and stained jacket he'd taken from the box of charity hand-me-downs.

"You usually dress better."

"I know, but it's laundry day. I'll fill you in at the same time I talk to Joe."

Sammy pulled into traffic. "I saw what was left of the van on the news. You're doing good just to be walking around."

"The hitters weren't Irish, they were Hispanic, maybe Salvadorans. I think there's a third player in the game."

"That's an interesting development, but what I want to know is how they knew you were in that van. Maybe you were followed?"

"Possible, but I smell a rat."

"We're going to the strip club. Uncle Joe will be there, and speaking of rats, Rico Nazario will be there too."

"I take it you're not a fan of Rico's?"

"I haven't forgotten that he was working for the man who killed Sophia. If it turns out that Rico is the traitor, he's mine, Tanner."

"I wouldn't have it any other way," Tanner said, before staring out the window and watching the early morning commute.

14

A FAVOR FOR A FRIEND

Sara broke into a huge grin as she opened her arms to give Alicia Kincaid a hug.

The two women had been close when they were teenagers but hadn't seen each other in over two years. Alicia Kincaid looked like a smaller version of Sara. Alicia's curves were less generous, her height several inches shorter, and yet, from the neck up they could pass for twins.

They caught up with what had been happening in their lives since they last saw each other. Sara's version of events was so edited and sanitized as to be a work of fiction. However, she did tell Alicia that she had gotten over Brian Ames untimely death, had left the FBI, and that she was in love with a man named Thomas Myers. Thomas Myers was the name that Tanner used as an alias, complete with passport, driver's license, birth certificate, and bank accounts.

The new identity had been given to Tanner by a genius computer hacker named Tim Jackson as a thank you for Tanner having saved his life.

Alicia owned a dance studio, was between lovers, and filled with concern for her younger brother, Kevin Kincaid, who was twenty, and a college student.

"What's wrong with Kevin? Is he ill?"

"No, Kevin's health is excellent. It's his judgement I'm worried about. Sara, he has money, and I mean a lot of money. I was over at his apartment one day recently and found thousands inside a garbage bag in a closet."

"A garbage bag?"

"Yes, and I wasn't snooping, I was cleaning. His girlfriend used to keep the place livable, but ever since Kevin broke up with her the apartment is a pigsty. I stop in every so often to clean."

"I know you, Alicia. You must have confronted him about it. What did Kevin have to say?"

Alicia took in a deep breath and held it as she fought back tears. When she spoke, Sara could hear the pain in her voice.

"He told me to mind my own business, demanded that I give him back the key he'd let me have, and now he refuses to talk about it."

"Has he been spending a lot of money lately, a new car, anything like that?"

"No, that's another thing. He's still the same typically broke college student as far as I can tell."

"Alicia, there's an obvious answer to how Kevin might have come by the money, you know?"

"I know what you're thinking Sara, but no, it couldn't be drugs. Not after what we all went through with Michael. Kevin would never have anything to do with the drug trade."

Sara nodded in understanding. Michael Kincaid had been the younger brother of Alicia and the older brother of Kevin.

He died a meth addict, but not before devastating his family. During his fifth trip to a treatment center, Michael Kincaid reached over the front seat and grabbed the steering wheel from his father's control, causing them to crash. He had been attempting to make a U-turn, instead, he flipped the car. The resulting injuries to his parents ultimately proved fatal, and they died only days apart. Michael had fled from the scene, unharmed, and never contacted his family again. Months later, his body was discovered after a meth lab exploded inside an abandoned building in Paterson, New Jersey.

"Okay, so if it's not drug money, it's likely still from an illegal source. If that's the case, Kevin could get himself into a lot of trouble with the law."

"I know, and that's why I wanted to speak with you. I have a favor to ask."

"Is this about my father? Because you know, he gave up practicing criminal law."

"No, Sara, you misunderstand. I want you to help. I want you to find out what Kevin is up to."

"Me? Why not hire a private investigator?"

"Because whatever they discover they might not keep to themselves, but you will."

Sara considered the request. She loved Alicia and had always thought of her as a good friend. Although they had drifted apart in recent years, she would like to help her if she could, and the truth was, she had nothing else to do. Her contract with the Burke corporation had expired, and although she had been working with Tanner recently, he was not a man who required an assistant. She needed something to do and solving the mystery of Kevin Kincaid's newfound wealth might even prove to be a challenge.

"I'll help, Alicia."

"Thank you, Sara. I can't stand by and watch Kevin ruin his life. He's all the family I have left."

"I'll do my best."

"What will you do, just follow Kevin around and see where he goes?"

"Not yet. I need more information."

"I've told you everything I know."

"That girlfriend of Kevin's you mentioned, what's her name and where can I find her?"

"Oh, you think she might know something?"

"I don't know, but it's a place to start."

Alicia looked heavenward, as if a prayer had been answered. "I feel better already."

"I can't make any promises. Kevin might be in so deep that no one can get him out."

"I understand, but I know you, Sara. When you put your mind to something, no one can stop you. It's why I came to you for help."

They spoke a while longer, then Sara stood and grabbed her purse, as she prepared to go off and locate Kevin Kincaid's old girlfriend.

"Sara?"

"Yes?"

"Please be careful. I love Kevin to death, but I couldn't bear it if helping me led to your getting hurt."

Sara's smile was full of hidden meaning. "Don't worry. I've been known to hold my own in a fight."

TANNER WAS WITH JOE PULLO INSIDE JOHNNY R'S. Gathered with them were Sammy, Bosco, and Rico Nazario. Tanner told them the story of the attack he faced on the highway. They were all in agreement that it sounded like they were leaking information somewhere.

"Who knew that I was going to Boston?" Tanner asked.

"Bosco, Sammy, and me," Joe said. "But others knew about the van we got for you to use, and Rico here was the one who came up with the Massachusetts plates."

"I vote we kill Rico," Sammy said.

Rico glared at Sammy. "If you do, you'll be killing an innocent man."

"I'm willing to take that risk."

"Enough with you two," Joe said. "Bosco, who else knew about the van?"

"It was delivered around the back, so Ivanov knew about it. Also, Red probably heard us talking about it in the limo."

Joe shook his head. "I can't buy either of them working with someone to kill Tanner."

"Whoever it was knew that I would be in the van, or saw me get into it, but I don't think they knew where I was headed or why."

Joe ran the back of his right hand along the stubble on the underside of his chin. He had left home at daybreak after getting Tanner's messages, and only took time for a quick shower.

"I really wanted to talk to that Sean O'Doyle," Joe said. "We could have made him confess that he was working under orders from Moss Murphy."

"Murphy wasn't behind the robbery of the bakery," Tanner said, then he went on to explain the conversation he had eavesdropped on between Sean O'Doyle and the man he heard but never saw.

"That sounds like Murphy doesn't know what's going on either," Joe said.

"Maybe you both have leaks," Rico said. "And Tanner, what makes you think that the men who tried to kill you were Salvadorans?"

"They were pretty mangled up by the time I got a close look at them, but at least two of them had face tattoos. The kind the Salvadoran gangs are known for."

Rico grimaced. "They wouldn't work for Moss Murphy or anyone else. If they're behind the robberies, it means they're making moves."

"And they wanted Tanner out of the way," Bosco said.

"They just ensured that I stay in. Whoever sent them after me will see me himself someday."

Joe held up a finger and caught Bosco's eye. "Tell Big Ralphie to stay on his toes, and put two men on Laurel, but loosely, I don't want her worried about why I'm upping the security around her."

"I'll take care of it, Joe, but can I suggest something?"

"That's why I keep you around, every once in a while, you come up with a good idea."

"Let me meet with Finn Kelly, Moss Murphy's number two man. He's always seemed like a straight shooter to me."

"You think he'll be willing to talk with you?"

"I don't know, but if he is, we might get some answers."

"Or you might get killed," Sammy said.

Bosco pursed his lips while shaking his head. "That's not Finn Kelly's style. If he agrees to meet it won't be a set up."

Joe nodded. "See if he'll meet you."

"I'll go make the call, but first, I'll see that Laurel gets more security."

"Good man," Joe said.

Bosco was gone for twenty minutes as Joe, Sammy,

Tanner, and Rico considered options. When Bosco returned, he wore an odd expression and had news.

"We've got new trouble."

"How's that?"

"One of our cocaine shipments was almost stolen in a warehouse at the docks. Three guys got away, but not with the drugs."

Joe stood in a rush. "They kill anyone?"

"No, but a man was shot in the arm."

"Who?"

"A kid named Adamo Conti. They say he wounded one of the heisters with a knife as he fought them off."

"Why a knife and not a gun?"

"They missed the knife when they patted Conti down. The kid used it to get back his gun, and that's when the heisters ran."

"When Conti recovers from the shooting, set up a meet here. That kid is getting moved up a notch, along with a bonus."

"Will do, and one more thing, these guys were white. Conti struggled with one and yanked his mask off."

"Maybe Moss Murphy is making moves, or someone wants me to think so."

"Could be someone wants New York and Boston to go to war so that they can pick up the pieces when the dust settles," Tanner said.

"There is good news, boss," Bosco said. "Moss Murphy himself agreed to meet with you."

"When and where?"

"At four o'clock. He wants to meet in Killburry, Connecticut."

"Maybe he'll hand the town back to us as a peace offering," Sammy said, but only as a joke.

"Tell them we'll be there, Bosco, all four of us."

"Make that five," Tanner said. "I want to be there."

Joe smiled. "Tell them five men apiece, Bosco."

After Bosco left to confirm the meet, Rico shrugged. "Maybe things will get settled."

Joe lowered himself into his chair again. "Or maybe all hell is about to break loose."

15
LET'S TALK

Sara sat at a table inside a department store. She was in the employee break room and having a conversation with the ex-girlfriend of Kevin Kincaid.

Emma Poole was blonde and pretty, with shoulder-length hair and green eyes. She worked the perfume counter part-time while going to college for a degree in engineering.

"Kevin has a lot of pent-up rage over what happened with his brother, Michael. Most of it is directed at the drug dealer who sold Michael the drugs."

"I wasn't aware the family knew who his dealer was."

"I don't think they have a name, and there was likely more than one. But Kevin hates all drug dealers. Once, when we were at a friend's party, Kevin got in a fight with a guy selling pot. You would have thought the guy was peddling child porn the way Kevin reacted. That was when I asked him to get help."

"By help, do you mean a psychiatrist?"

Emma sat her coffee cup down on the table. "I meant a group. People like Kevin who had also lost family members due to drug use. I know from experience that talking things out with like-minded people can be healing. It worked for me, concerning the abuse I suffered as a child, I thought it might help Kevin too."

"I take it he wouldn't go?"

"He went. He found a group through the college and started attending regularly. But see, instead of helping Kevin, he seemed to become more obsessed."

"How so?"

"I would watch him search the web for stories about drug dealers who'd been busted but placed back on the streets. It infuriated Kevin. By the time we broke up, Kevin was walking around campus with a petition to have the drug laws toughened. He and his group wanted the laws changed so that anyone selling or buying drugs would receive the death penalty. Miss Blake, almost no one signed it."

"You say the group was a part of the petition. I thought the purpose of a support group was to help the members deal with their emotional difficulties, not turn them into activists."

Emma Poole's eyes grew large as she nodded agreement. "Exactly, and now I wish Kevin had never joined that group. It changed him."

Sara wrote down the name of the group and the names of the members Emma knew. There was the group's founder and leader, Ian Seagate. Seagate was in his late-thirties and a law professor. There were also three fellow students whom Kevin had grown close to, Roland, whom Emma said was blond, stick thin, and nervous. Gabriel, with dark hair, dark eyes, and walked with a limp. Then there was Juan Vega, Kevin's new best friend. Vega was good-looking and drove a vintage sports car that he'd saved for since he was twelve.

"How many more members are in the group?" Sara asked.

"That might be all of them. Professor Seagate is arrogant and tends to rub people the wrong way, but Kevin sure likes him. He thought the man could do no wrong."

"Why did you and Kevin break up?"

Emma pushed a strand of hair from her eyes. "It just wasn't much fun to be around him anymore, and he was spending most of his time with the group."

"I see."

"Miss Blake, are you related to Kevin."

Sara smiled. "No, I just happen to resemble his sister."

"You really do, and Kevin too."

Sara asked a few more questions and walked with Emma as she returned to the perfume counter. As they were saying goodbye, Emma asked a question.

"Is Kevin in trouble, Miss Blake?"

"That's what I'm going to find out."

IN KILLBURRY, CONNECTICUT, TANNER CLIMBED OUT OF the rear of a limo with Joe, Sammy, and Rico, as Bosco got out of the driver's seat.

The area they were in showed signs of its recent devastation. It was the site of Tanner's battle with the Brotherhood. Many of the homes had been destroyed by fire.

Not far away, Moss Murphy left his own limo with his son, Liam, his number two man, Finn Kelly, two young punks, and a mountain. At least, the man looked like a mountain. The red-haired giant was so huge that he made the twin black bouncers back at Johnny R's look small in comparison.

"What the hell is that?" Rico said.

Bosco laughed. "They call him the Irish hulk. He's their version of Big Ralphie."

Joe walked with Tanner beside him. The suit he wore was blue, the tie, red, while Tanner's suit was black and unaccompanied by a tie. Both men had their jackets unbuttoned.

"Let's go see where this takes us," Joe said.

The two groups headed toward each other and met in the street before a pile of debris that had once been the home of Burt Hodges, Killburry's former head mobster. Killburry's current criminal mastermind was Liam Murphy. Murphy was as handsome as his father, who was a notorious ladies man. Liam was dressed in tight black jeans, red sneakers, and wore a white T-shirt under a black leather jacket.

There was a gun on his left hip, a Glock, and that side of the jacket was pushed back to make the weapon easier to extract. Liam Murphy was a stone-cold punk, but he was a punk who enjoyed the clout and backing of his powerful father.

Liam was looking at Tanner the way a talented young boxer eyed an undefeated champion. It was a hungry look, and a cocky one. Brashness and danger danced together in Liam Murphy's blue eyes.

Finn Kelly, Murphy's number two man, was the opposite of Liam. He was about Tanner's age or perhaps a few years younger, wore glasses with thin black frames, and his gray eyes looked as calm and flat as a lake on a windless day. If asked, most people would have guessed that Finn Kelly was an accountant, or perhaps a dentist. No one would claim he was a mobster.

When Tanner's gaze met Kelly's, the Irishman sent

him a slight nod of acknowledgement, and Tanner answered with the same.

After everyone had eyed everyone else, with the Irish hulk and Tanner getting most of the stares, Joe tossed his chin in Moss Murphy's direction.

"I thought we agreed on five men apiece? I count six on your side."

Murphy shrugged. "I didn't think we were counting ourselves in that."

"You don't consider yourself a man?" Sammy asked Murphy.

Moss Murphy turned his gaze on Sammy. "Who the fuck are you?"

"I'm Sammy Giacconi."

"Ah, the grandson. I didn't know you had a mouth on you."

"Now you do," Sammy said.

Liam spoke up, while looking at Tanner. He was moving a lot, twitching, as if trying to disperse nervous energy.

"You're Tanner, right?"

"Yeah."

"How fast are you?"

Tanner watched the kid. "What do you mean?"

"On the draw, you know, with a gun. How fast can you draw a gun?"

"Fast enough."

"You're supposed to be this big fucking deal, but you don't look like much."

"We can't all be as pretty as you, kid."

"Yeah, I'm pretty. The bitches love my ass. I'm fast too, Tanner. I'm the fastest fucking gun in Boston."

"Liam!" Moss Murphy said in a warning tone. His son flashed a glance his way, then spoke to Tanner again.

"Why don't we find out who's faster?"

"I thought we were here to talk."

Liam laughed, as his hand crept closer to the gun on his hip. "Hear that, everybody? Fucking Tanner just came here to talk. I think he's scared."

"Murphy," Joe said. "Put a choke chain on your boy before he winds up dead."

"Liam! Leave Tanner the fuck alone. He's right, we came here to talk."

Murphy's tone had been harsher, but this time, Liam didn't even give his father the courtesy of a glance. He was smiling at Tanner, as he pretended to go for his gun, then stopped his hand only inches away from it. Bosco, Sammy, and Rico looked to be on edge by Liam's antics, but Joe and Tanner simply observed the show.

It turned out that Liam hadn't been boasting. The kid was fast, just lightning quick. However, others were faster.

Liam's gun was halfway out of his holster when three things occurred within hundreds of a second of each other. Tanner, along with Joe, had cleared leather, and they were pointing their guns at the boy. Meanwhile, Finn Kelly had reached over and grabbed Liam's wrist, to prevent him from drawing his weapon. Liam struggled against Kelly's grasp, but it was no use, the man was too strong for him.

Bosco, Sammy, Rico, and the two street soldiers from Boston all stood with their hands on their guns while looking at each other with nervous eyes. The man-mountain that was the Irish Hulk maneuvered his bulk in front of Moss Murphy, thus, keeping the man safe behind a wall of flesh.

Liam was staring at Joe and Tanner in astonishment. He was fast, knew he was fast, but the men before him were on a whole other level. If Finn Kelly hadn't prevented him from clearing his holster, he would be on the ground bleeding. Still, punk that he was, Liam reacted with anger and petulance.

"Take your fucking hand off me, Finn!"

Kelly removed his hand, but slowly, while berating Liam. Kelly's voice had the lilt of an Irish accent. Tanner realized he was listening to the man who had been at Sean O'Doyle's apartment the night before. Finn Kelly had questioned Sean O'Doyle about the robbery at the bakery.

"That was a stupid thing to do, Liam. You're lucky Tanner and Mr. Pullo didn't blow your fool head off."

"My father told you not to talk to me that way."

"You're right. He also told you to leave Tanner alone. You'd be best to heed that advice, boy."

Tanner and Joe holstered their weapons much slower than they had brought them out.

Liam scowled at Tanner, his eyes now devoid of their earlier devilishness. The brashness had been replaced by a guarded gaze.

"Let's talk about business now, hmm?" Joe said.

The others all relaxed, except for Tanner and Finn Kelly, because neither man's pulse rate had risen during the incident. Tanner took note of Kelly's calmness, along with the speed he displayed when he grabbed Liam's wrist. He classified the bland Irishman as the only true threat before them.

Moss Murphy stepped out from behind his human shield, scowled at his son, but then smiled at Joe.

"I'm glad you came. I don't think either of us wants war."

"That's a funny thing to say while you're standing on turf you took without asking."

Liam pointed at the ground. "Hey Pullo, this town was up for grabs after the Brotherhood got their asses fried in a fire."

"I started that fire," Tanner said. "I didn't do it so the Boston mob could just roll in here like homeless squatters."

Moss Murphy smiled as he raised up his hands and patted the air. He looked like a politician trying to placate an angry crowd. "It's all in the past. That's the main thing I came here to say. As of today, we're leaving Killburry."

"What's the catch?" Joe said.

"There's no catch, Joe, and no reason for us to fight."

"Uh-huh, so I take it you won't be sending any more Sean O'Doyle's my way?"

"O'Doyle was a maverick."

"A maverick?"

"Yeah, you know, like a troublemaker. I even had Kelly question him because I suspected he might have been behind that bakery robbery. But hey, I didn't send him. Anyway, like I said, it's all in the past."

Joe pointed at Tanner. "It's not, 'all in the past.' Some crew of Salvadorans went after Tanner early this morning. What do you know about that?"

Murphy's smile faltered. "What would I be doing dealing with Salvadorans? And you say they went after Tanner? Then that would mean that Tanner was the one who grabbed O'Doyle out of Boston, *my* turf."

"I was cleaning up your maverick problem for you," Tanner said. "But there's no need to thank me."

Murphy's smile disappeared, and in truth, it had never reached the level of his eyes. He looked over at his son as if he could strangle the boy. Tanner wondered what voiceless message had just passed between them.

"Joe," Murphy said, trying to sound calm. "Let's put this trouble behind us. I have no idea why Tanner was attacked, but the man does have enemies."

"Never for long," Tanner said.

Pullo took a step closer to Murphy. "We got hit four

times, Moss, and we lost the revenue from this town. Before anything is settled, we need to talk about compensation."

Murphy's smile returned. "It's done. When I said I wanted to put this in the past, I meant it. Have your man Bosco there call Kelly with a figure, and I'll pay it."

"Just like that?"

"Yes, Joe. C'mon, how long have we known each other? Have we ever had trouble before?"

"Nothing like this."

Murphy spread his hands. "That's right, and we both have businesses to run. I don't want to fight a war. I just want to make a shitload of money and bang as many women as I can."

Tanner was looking at Kelly. For just a second, he saw a look of disapproval replace the bland expression.

"Bosco," Joe said. "Give 'em a ballpark figure on our losses."

Bosco named a number and Moss Murphy didn't even blink.

"You got it. We'll put this crap in the past and move forward. We'll call and arrange the when and where for the money pick up. Anything else?"

"Just this, anymore shit goes down and it's war."

Murphy nodded. "Sure Joe, whatever you say, and now that we've made peace, neither of us will have any more trouble."

Joe was sure Murphy was just humoring him by agreeing, but he knew it didn't matter. "I guess we're done," he said.

"Enjoy Killburry, Joe, but don't expect to make a fortune. The law here is tough on crooks like us."

"Yeah, see you around, Moss."

The groups separated again and went back to their

respective limos. One of Moss Murphy's punks drove while the other one sat in the passenger seat. In the rear of the limo, Moss Murphy was facing ahead. He was seated on the right with his son beside him and Finn Kelly on the left. Across from them sat the Irish hulk, who took up the entire bench seat.

"We should have laid our cards on the table, Moss. Pullo and Tanner make good allies, but deadly enemies."

"It's too late for that, Kelly, after what Liam has done."

Liam made a face of displeasure. "You keep bitching about it, but it was the right move. That old-school Mafia shit is over, and the street gangs are growing bigger every day. It's better to be a part of a team than to have those bastards run us over."

"It wasn't your decision to make, Liam."

"Why not? Are you going to live forever? I'm the future, Dad, not you, and so far, my plan has worked."

Finn Kelly shook his head in wonder at Liam's arrogance. "Your plan? If your plan was to be a gutless wonder and rollover for some street gang, then yeah, boy, your plan worked."

"You can't talk to me that way, tell him, Dad."

"Liam's right, Kelly, show my boy some respect or I'll have you put down."

Kelly blinked in surprise. "Moss, I've done nothing but look out for you for years, and I'm telling you now, Liam will be the ruin of you. If you go ahead with your plans, Tanner will turn Boston into a graveyard."

Moss Murphy swiveled his head slowly until he was staring at Kelly. "I don't want to hear any more about it. Pullo and Tanner have to die. New York City is the price the Salvadorans asked to leave us alone."

"They won't stay out of Boston once they control New York. Don't you see that?"

"We'll deal with it then. Now stop talking."

"But Moss—"

"Enough!"

Kelly said nothing more. He fought the urge to smash Liam's face, as the punk smiled and gave him the finger.

As Bosco drove back toward the freeway, Sammy asked a question.

"Am I the only one who thinks Moss Murphy is full of shit?"

"I didn't buy that act for a second," Joe said.

"He'll come after you soon, Joe," Rico said, "but he'll wait until you drop your guard."

"What do you think, Tanner?" Joe asked.

"Rico's right, Murphy will make a move on you, but I think it's because he can't handle his son. That boy writes big checks, but it's his father who has to cash them."

Joe made a face of disgust that revealed his irritation. "That dumb bastard. The last thing we should be doing is fighting among ourselves. There's a hundred new gangs coming up that want our turf."

"Like the Mexican cartels," Sammy said, while glaring at Rico.

Rico ignored him, and no one said anything for a time, while Joe looked lost in thought.

"Joe."

"Yeah, Tanner?"

"Just say the word."

Joe was quiet, but then sighed. "I can't order a hit on him. Not after we just settled things. That would make the Giacconi Family the ones who started the war."

"I still believe that either Murphy or his son was

behind the attack on me last night. I'll be paying them a visit whether you order a hit or not."

"It will still look like I ordered the hit."

"I won't kill him, for now, but I think I'll return to Boston tomorrow."

"Why?"

"For planning purposes. When Murphy makes a move, I want to be ready to hit him."

"There may be an army protecting him."

"True, but no one's protecting them."

"Uncle Joe," Sammy said. "I'll cancel my trip to New Orleans. The hell with Ricky Valente."

"No, kid, go take care of that. It's bad business to let that bastard get away."

"You're sure?"

"Catch that plane, a change of scenery may do you some good."

"All right, but I'll get back as soon as I can."

"Tanner, when you're in Boston, keep an eye out for that Finn Kelly," Joe said. "I think he's the real deal."

"Agreed," Tanner said, as the limo rolled back toward New York.

16

I SPY

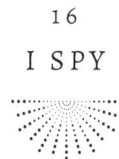

Sara watched Kevin Kincaid's car enter the long and graveled driveway of a house in Tarrytown, New York. Tarrytown was a village about thirty miles north of New York City.

Sara drove by the house, as there was nowhere to park on the road and several cars were behind her. According to Emma Poole, Kevin's ex-girlfriend, the house belonged to Ian Seagate, a thirty-nine-year-old law professor.

Seagate and his fiancée bought the three-acre property seven years ago. It had a rambling old house and a dilapidated barn. The couple had planned to tear down the house and build a new home, but Seagate's fiancée was killed by a stray bullet fired by a drug dealer. The man had been defending himself during an attempted robbery by a rival dealer. Seagate was on the scene when it happened, and it occurred six days before the wedding.

Sara pulled over onto the shoulder a half mile down the road. When the way was clear moments later, she drove across the two-lane thoroughfare to park at a farm stand that was closed for the season. She was facing the way she had come and could see the mouth of Seagate's driveway.

Once she obtained a satellite image of the property on her phone, Sara saw that the old house sat well back from the road. Even from the overhead view you could tell that the house had seen better days. Seagate didn't live there; he had a home in Brooklyn.

Two more cars went up Seagate's driveway. One was a common economy car in blue, but the other was an old Chevy Camaro in showroom condition. Sara could see the car's bright red paint job sparkle in the sun. Five more minutes passed before another car appeared, and it contained the last of their group. Supposedly, they were meeting there for a therapy session, but then, why not meet on campus? It was a long drive and the college had facilities for groups to gather.

Something other than therapy was going on inside that old house, something profitable, and perhaps illegal. Sara kept one eye on the driveway while she searched the web to find out everything she could about Professor Ian Seagate.

INSIDE THE BARN ON HIS PROPERTY, IAN SEAGATE WAS grinning with pride at his young friends as they all tapped fists together. The plan was working. They were doing something about their problems instead of just talking endlessly about them, and in a few days, his sweet Emily would be avenged.

Seagate had devised the plan, had revealed it to a select few, then they had sat around perfecting it. Of course, it had all been just a game back then, just a mental exercise about extracting justice from a broken system.

Seagate knew the name of the drug dealer who'd fired

the shot that killed his fiancée. He also knew that the sonofabitch walked out of the courtroom with a reduced sentence after he testified against his suppliers. The man had been arrested on numerous charges, including homicide, for causing the death of Seagate's bride-to-be, Emily. The bottom line was that the man who killed Emily was walking around free, having just been released a week earlier. The bastard had only served six years. But that would change after tomorrow, and the plan would be completed.

The plan was bold and required that they themselves break the law, but even that served a sense of justice. The bank branches they robbed all belonged to the same Megabank, a corporation that had been tied to money laundering the drug profits of a Mexican cartel.

They had robbed four banks over the last few months in different sections of the city. Each robbery had a different M.O. and no one was injured. After each robbery, the money found its way into the possession of a known drug dealer. So far, all four men faced bank robbery charges and were serving time in prison or awaiting sentencing while in jail. None of the dealers had a direct tie to the group. Of the group's five members, only Seagate knew who to blame for his loss, while also having an opportunity to take revenge on the man.

Seagate smiled at the young men before him. There was Roland, 18, blond, stick thin, and nervous. Roland had lost a sister to meth. Gabriel, 20, with dark hair and dark eyes. Gabriel walked with a limp. He had been shot in the hip by the same drug dealer who'd killed his parents. The man had riddled their car with bullets. Gabriel's father had been mistaken for a police informant. That drug dealer was dead, killed in a shootout with the cops, but Gabriel still held hate for the bastard. However, after framing a similar man for one of their bank robberies, Gabriel said it made him feel better. At least they had swept one piece of garbage off the streets.

Seagate's smile widened as he looked at Juan Vega. Vega was 19, Mexican, smart, and good-looking. He was a Christian and wanted to be a preacher. His stories about living life in a cartel-controlled town had sent shivers through the group. His mother came to the states with Juan and his two older sisters when he was twelve. They fled their country to escape the random drug violence that had taken the life of Juan's father.

Then, there was Kevin Kincaid. The dark-haired college senior was filled with righteous anger about the devastation that drug addiction had brought to his family.

They were still boys really, Seagate knew, but they had each suffered a loss because of drugs. Each could pick a target to go after, like their latest, a no-good piece of crap named Tony Zade. Zade had been Juan Vega's choice, because the man sold drugs in Juan's building.

The police arrested Zade for their last robbery, but tomorrow Ian Seagate would finally get the justice he craved, and then the plan would be complete. It was more than justice. They were committing a series of perfect crimes.

Kevin approached Seagate while gesturing at a green van that was parked inside the barn. "Everything is ready, Professor. Juan switched out the license plates on the van and everything we need tomorrow is in the back of it."

"Great, I'll return here early tomorrow and drive the van into the city. Once the last bank robbery is completed, you'll be driving me back here."

"What if the man we're framing is with people who can give him an alibi?"

"That's why Gabriel will be keeping an eye on him. If

we must postpone the robbery, we'll do so, but I doubt it. I've been watching that bastard off and on since he was released from prison. All he ever does is stay inside that rooming house he lives in."

"And Juan will see to our distraction," Kevin said, then grinned. "We should do more of these and not stop after tomorrow."

Seagate held up a finger, as a gesture of caution. "No, that would be pushing our luck."

"You're right, it's just that, I don't know. It's all gone so smoothly that I can't see anything going wrong."

LUIS ZADE ENTERED HIS BROTHER'S APARTMENT IN THE Bronx and told the moving men accompanying him to just pack up everything. He would place it in storage and worry about it later. Luis's brother, Tony, was going to prison for years. While Luis was a professional thief, Tony was a drug dealer.

Recently, the police had entered Tony's apartment with a warrant. When they left, Tony was in cuffs and charged with possession and intent to sell. That wasn't surprising, but what was shocking is that Tony was also charged with bank robbery. Tony swore to Luis on their mother's soul that he didn't rob the bank. However, the money from a recent bank robbery was discovered in the apartment.

The money had been placed in the freezer and hidden inside a TV dinner that was years old.

Luis believed his brother, which meant that Tony had been framed, but the cops didn't give a damn and kept hounding Tony to give up his partners.

The newspaper accounts of the robbery claimed the police believed the bank was robbed by a five-man team.

Two of them caused a distraction on the street, while the other three entered the bank dressed like Santa Claus, as the robbery took place only days before Christmas.

Tony had been framed, but he had no clue who would have done it. The crowd he ran with were drug merchants, not bank robbers. Luis told Tony that he would look into it and keep searching. If he ever found out who framed his brother, he would kill them. It was as simple as that.

Sara watched the last car leave Seagate's property and checked the time on her dashboard. She would be running late for her dinner with Tanner, so she sent off a text. When he texted her back saying that he was running late as well, she wondered what he was doing, but when he mentioned that he would be meeting a man named Duke later, Sara knew that something big was up.

Duke was a specialist in procurement. The man had contacts in many fields of interest and social strata. Tanner had met Duke through Sara, but only used the man's services when he faced a serious situation.

Worry creased her brow only for an instant. Whatever it was, Tanner would handle it.

After considering the pluses and minuses, Sara decided to be bold and just drive up to Ian Seagate's house. She was all but certain that no one was still there. Even if there were someone around, she could just claim to have the wrong address.

The house was larger than it looked online, while also appearing in need of either a total renovation or a wrecking ball. The doors were all locked, which was to be expected, but a rear door of the old barn wasn't. Inside the barn was where Sara found items of interest.

There was a panel van inside, and inside that three bicycles, three backpacks, and three bright orange bike helmets. After picking up one of the helmets, Sara saw that the orange covering would peel off easily, revealing the white color beneath it. Sara pondered the significance of such camouflage as she placed the helmet back and closed the van. It was getting dark, and the unlit barn was growing deep shadows.

She saw nothing else of interest and drove away from the house. Tomorrow she would follow Kevin around again, because it was all she could think to do. Kevin and his group were up to something. Sara was certain of that much. She wouldn't quit poking around until she figured out the mystery.

Luis Zade closed the door on Tony's empty apartment and saw a young woman coming up the stairs.

She was Tony's neighbor, as well as a customer who bought a line of coke now and then. Her name was Shawna, and she was just getting home from work. Tony never said so, but Luis suspected that his brother and the married Shawna may have had a brief affair.

"Luis, hi, have you talked to Tony since his arrest?"

"Yeah, and he was framed, Shawna." Luis threw a thumb back at his brother's apartment. "Someone placed that money in there. You know Tony, he didn't rob any damn bank."

"I didn't believe it either, but framed? Who would give up all the money like that? He could have been framed with just a few bills, and whoever did it could keep the rest."

Luis's mouth opened slightly, as an idea struck him.

"You're right, Shawna. Who would do that? I think whoever framed Luis did it like a vigilante thing. You know, some holier than thou type that wouldn't dream of keeping the money for themselves."

Shawna was nodding. "I know the type. There's one in the building, a Mexican kid who's like a holy roller or something. He wears this big silver cross around his neck, but he drives an old red sports car."

"This boy ever give Tony any shit?"

Shawna smirked. "Not to Tony's face, but he would badmouth him in the lobby. I've heard him."

"What's his name?"

"Juan? Or maybe it's José, I'm not sure."

"Where's he work, do you know?"

"He's a college kid. Him and his mother live up on the fifth floor. Why? Are you going to kick his ass?"

"A punk like that wouldn't have the balls to frame my brother."

"No, he wouldn't, and he'd have to rob a bank first to do it."

Zade turned toward the stairs. "Thanks Shawna, and you take care."

"Luis."

Zade turned back to look at her. "Yeah?"

A smile crept over Shawna's lips as she looked him over. "My husband works nights on the weekend. Why don't you stop by and keep me company sometime?"

"I'll do that."

"All right then, and tell Tony I said hi."

Shawna went inside her apartment as Zade went down the stairs to the street. Once outside, he heard a car's throaty engine before he saw it. It was an old Camaro in primo condition, and a Mexican kid was behind the wheel.

When the traffic light changed, and the car was parked

near the apartment house, Zade knew he was looking at the boy he'd just been discussing with Shawna. Zade marched over, opened the passenger door, and slid in.

The kid was startled by Zade's appearance in his vehicle, and Zade decided to shake him up a little more, just to see what would happen.

"I know you framed my brother, you little shit, so don't even try to bullshit me."

The kid licked his lips, then spoke in a shaky voice. "You're Tony Zade's brother. You look like him."

"Why did you frame him, bitch?"

Zade expected denial, a shocked or confused look, or maybe a threat to call the police. He never expected what occurred next.

Juan Vega cried as he held the cross hanging from his neck. "I'm sorry."

"You did frame him? How, and who with? The papers said five people robbed the bank."

Juan wiped at his eyes. "I can't tell you. They're my friends."

Zade took out his gun and pointed it at Juan. "Kid, you're gonna tell me everything."

17

DUKE OF LOVE

In Manhattan, Tanner was inside a restaurant and sitting with Duke at the bar.

Tanner had called Duke earlier in the day and requested information on Moss Murphy. Duke had gotten that info, and as they sat together, Tanner looked over the layout of Moss Murphy's home. When you added the sixteen acres surrounding it, the place was more like an estate.

"As a bonus, I called a contact I have in the area. He told me that Moss Murphy gave the order for more troops to guard the house. He didn't know how many men would be guarding the man, but said it was in the dozens."

"That's good work, Duke, now I'm going to need some other things."

Duke took out a small notepad. "What do you need?"

"A UFO."

"Huh?"

"I need a UFO, an Unidentified Flying Object, and it has to be big."

Duke hesitated for only a moment before taking out his

laptop and looking at his contact list. "Do you need the thing to fly, you know, like a drone?"

"Yes, but I also need to be able to operate it with something no bigger than a TV remote."

"Give me a few minutes. I might know just the right guy."

"That's your business model, knowing the right guy."

"Or gal," Duke said. "Also, I don't ask too many questions."

"Is that why you haven't asked why I want a flying saucer?"

"It's none of my business, and I've dealt with stranger requests than this."

"I believe that."

Duke took out his phone and Tanner ordered them both a second round of beers. A few minutes later, Duke swung his laptop around and showed Tanner a short video of a realistic-looking flying saucer. It appeared to be large, maybe twelve feet across, and six-foot-high in the center, tapering down to a foot high at the edges.

"It works by remote control. And hear the sound? It's like something out of a movie, right?"

"Yeah, is that what it is, a movie prop?"

"It was built by a special effects guy in LA for a movie that never got made. They also never paid him for the work."

"Let me see that video again."

Duke started the video as his phone vibrated. "It's a text from my guy. He checked, and he can modify it to do what you want, but it eats battery power like crazy. It will only stay up in the air for about twenty minutes, and you'll need to practice with it."

Tanner watched the video again while Duke spoke. "Did you tell him he won't be getting it back?"

Duke angled his phone toward Tanner. "Yes, and here's his price. The damn thing must be made of gold."

Tanner pointed at the screen. "Those little alien mannequins he's got propped up around it, how much would he want for those, and will they fit inside the craft?"

"Just a second and I'll ask him." It took seventy-four seconds, but Duke had an answer. "They'll fit, but their weight will cut into your fly time, and he wants two grand apiece for them."

"Done, and I need it all here by tomorrow morning."

"The greedy bastard will want more for that, you know?"

"Pay it, and I'll need a place to practice with it."

"I know a spot, no charge. Anything else?"

Tanner nodded. "Oh yeah."

Sara joined Tanner and Duke as the two men were finishing their business. When Duke saw her kiss Tanner in greeting, his eyes grew wide, but he said nothing about it.

"Hello, Duke. How have you been?"

"I'm good, Sara, but I gotta get going. Tanner has just given me a lot of work."

"Duke?"

"Yeah?"

"Aren't you surprised that Tanner and I are together?"

"That would be an understatement."

"Then how come you didn't say anything?"

"Because it's none of my business."

Sara smiled. "I think I've missed you, Duke."

"Same here, honey, and Tanner, I'll see you tomorrow morning."

They moved to a table and ordered dinner. Sara looked as if she'd had a long day.

"I want to get a hotel room for the night, Tanner. I'm tired of driving back to Connecticut."

"That works for me, and Joe is lining up an apartment for us to look at."

Over dinner, they talked about their days. After Sara described what she'd found inside the van, Tanner offered an answer.

"It sounds like they're going to dress up like bicycle messengers."

"You're right, but why?"

"Maybe they're running a con game of some sort. You should ask the kid about it."

"I will if I don't discover what they're doing soon, but I don't think Kevin will talk to me. He knows I would tell his sister everything."

"You say he had a lot of money but doesn't appear to spend any of it, that's odd. Maybe he's being blackmailed."

"Maybe, but it still doesn't explain where the money came from in the first place."

"I could have a talk with that professor if you'd like."

Sara laughed. "A talk, hmm? Would that talk involve broken bones?"

Tanner smiled. "Maybe just a finger or two, but I would get answers."

"I appreciate the offer, but I think I'll handle this my way."

"Fine, but I'm a phone call away."

Sara took Tanner's hand in her own. "Please be careful with this Boston situation. I saw that van on the news and wondered how you survived the attack."

"I'll be fine. And that attack happened because there's a joker somewhere in the deck of cards called the Giacconi

Family. Someone is leaking information to Boston, and it looks like Boston may be in bed with a street gang."

"And meeting with Duke tonight, what was that about?"

"Preparations for war. If I need to hit Moss Murphy, first I'll have to get past a small army."

"I'm a phone call away too. Remember that."

"I do."

Once they finished their meal, Sara asked Tanner if he wanted dessert. After his eyes roamed over her body, he answered.

"I think I'd like a taste of something else."

Sara laughed. "And I think I know what that might be."

They left the restaurant, after skipping dessert, and went looking for a room for the night.

IN TARRYTOWN, LUIS ZADE WAS LOOKING INSIDE THE green van that Sara had been searching earlier. He was with Juan Vega, who was a little worse for wear after being interrogated. Juan had told Zade everything, about all the bank robberies and the men they framed for them, including Zade's brother, Tony.

Zade would have been willing to go against his nature and involve the police if he thought for a second it would help Tony avoid doing any more time. But Tony already had a record when they arrested him and was going up on enough drug charges so that it didn't matter.

His lawyer was working a deal on the charges, so they'd run concurrently. Ten years for the drug charges, ten years for the bank job, but you serve the sentences together. So, ten years was ten years, and handing Juan Vega and his friends over to the cops wouldn't mean a thing. On the other hand, if they went through with the next robbery, Zade could rip them off for the money, then get payback.

Zade slammed the van door shut and saw Juan jump in fright. He had played the bad cop with the kid, now it was time to play the good cop.

"Yo, Juan, let's get back in the car. It's chilly in here."

They moved along in the darkness by navigating with light from their cell phones. Once they were back in Juan's car, Zade let out a great sigh.

"What am I gonna do with you, Juan?"

The boy said nothing, but he kept a hand over his stomach. Zade had punched him in the midsection twice as incentive to talk.

"I could call the police, but that wouldn't help my brother, not with all the drugs they found in his apartment. And those other guys you framed, I don't give a damn about them."

Juan's chin lifted off his chest, as in his mind, a light was seen at the end of a tunnel.

"You're not going to call the police?"

"I might, but really, why bother? That professor should have known better than to fuck with people, but you and those other kids you told me about, you're still young. A prison record would screw up your lives. I need to think about this."

Juan raised his head higher and swallowed hard. "I don't want to go to prison."

Zade had to resist the urge to smash the boy's face in. The little prick was whining about going to prison when he sent Tony and other guys up for years. It would be a pleasure to kill him, but first, he had to play nice.

"I have to admit it; you dudes were clever. Do you think the robbery will work tomorrow?"

"It would have, yeah, and Professor Seagate says that branch has a lot of money on hand. The wholesale merchants in that area still handle a lot of cash."

"Did he know how much you guys would get?"

"Not really, but it could be more than twenty thousand dollars behind the counter."

"Hmm," Zade said. "That would make a nice payday." Afterward, he waited to see if the kid would come up with the idea, or whether he'd have to suggest it.

"Mr. Zade… I'm sorry that I set up your brother."

"Your friends will be sorry too."

"You don't have to turn us in."

"Why shouldn't I? Where's the downside for me?"

After nearly a minute went by in silence, Zade figured the kid wasn't bright enough to see his best move, but no, he figured it out.

"I could give you the money."

"What money? The cops have all of it."

"No, I mean from tomorrow's robbery. I won't tell the others that you know about us until after we rob the bank. Then I'll tell them and make them give you the money."

"Will they do it?"

Juan was grinning. "Yeah, they'll have to, or you'll call the police, but if you take the money, then it's like you're one of us."

"Hmm, that could work, and it would make us even."

"Right, right, just come here tomorrow after two o'clock. That's when Kevin Kincaid will show up with the cash from the bank robbery."

"What's Kincaid look like?"

"If you give me my phone back I can show you pictures of everybody."

Zade handed Juan the phone. The kid had a lot of

pictures of himself and the Kincaid boy. Zade pointed at one of the photos. "Are you two homos?"

"What? No, but he's my best friend."

Zade pointed at another picture. It showed Juan and Kevin with a good-looking woman. She was dressed in a leotard.

"Who's the hottie with you in this picture?"

"That's Kevin's sister, Alicia."

"Is she a dancer?"

"She was for a while, but now she owns a dance studio and teaches little girls how to do ballet."

Zade pointed at the barn. "Will everyone meet in there or at that old house?"

"We always use the barn."

"All right, kid, we have a deal. But don't tell the others, or they might call off the robbery."

"I won't say anything until you show up. After that, they'll see that it makes sense to give you the money."

"Okay then, drive us back to the apartment house."

"It's a good thing my mom is working the four to midnight shift today, otherwise, she'd be wondering where I was."

Zade smiled. Before long, the kid's mother would always know where to find him. He'd be in the grave, along with his friends.

18

LIKE A KING AND A QUEEN

The following morning, Tanner went to Johnny R's after meeting with Duke.

Duke had delivered everything Tanner had asked for, including the UFO. Tanner practiced flying the movie prop in an airplane hangar in New Jersey that was scheduled to be torn down and replaced.

The machine's controller was small and could be hidden in a pocket. One side had buttons for basic functions, while the other side was a small view screen for the cameras. The UFO had been created to hover in a pattern without an operator at the controls once it was airborne. When Tanner had the proper maneuver input into the machine, he practiced working the cameras.

Before leaving the airport, Tanner went over the truck he would use for transport. It was old, but it would make it to the Boston area, and that's all Tanner needed.

Duke separated from Tanner a happy man after receiving a bonus, and Tanner was satisfied that he could get to Moss Murphy, regardless of how many men protected him.

Tanner sat at the bar and talked to Tamir Ivanov. The strip club didn't open until four in the afternoon, which was a later start time than the club's predecessor, the Cabaret Strip Club. Joe wanted Johnny R's to cater to a more well-heeled crowd and ditched the lunch hours.

Red had been seated at the bar when Tanner sat down. Red eyed Tanner with a worried look, as if Tanner might shoot him at any moment, just to keep in practice.

"They call you Red, right?"

"Yes sir, Mr. Tanner."

"Just call me Tanner, kid."

"Yes sir."

Tanner turned from the kid and spoke to Ivanov. "This is the last place I ever thought I'd see you."

"Retirement was boring, Tanner, and after what I did last year, I could no longer wear a badge."

"Joe says you're a natural at running a strip club."

"My father had a bar, no girls, but a tavern is a tavern."

Red walked around the bar to get a refill of soda, but he ducked out of sight when Gina Rossetti walked off the elevator. When Gina spotted Tanner, she went over and sat beside him.

"Hello, Mr. Tanner, it's nice to see you again."

"Same here."

Gina smiled. "If even half the things I've heard about you are true, you're an interesting man."

"It's all lies," Tanner said, as he wondered if the girl was flirting with him.

Gina placed a hand on his arm. "You have unusual eyes. Are there any other parts of you that are unique?"

"Yes, but it's not as easy to see as my eyes."

Gina's own eyes drifted downward, to stare at his

crotch. Tanner realized that Gina Rossetti was no innocent when it came to men.

"Hmm, maybe I'll get a look at this other body part someday."

"Why not now?" Tanner said.

Gina's smile became lopsided. "Right here?"

"Sure." Tanner opened his mouth and pointed at a back tooth. "See that, I have an extra molar on that side."

Behind the bar, Ivanov was smiling, but Gina stared at Tanner with an odd look.

"Are you making fun of me?"

"No."

"I was just being nice to you."

"I know."

"I heard something else about you, that you're dating my brother's old girlfriend."

"Correct."

"I never met her. What's she like?"

"She's as beautiful as you are, and smart too."

"Mrs. Pullo doesn't like her."

"I know."

Gina smiled again. "Laurel likes you… maybe too much."

"We're friends."

"Um-hmm," Gina said while standing. She held up a key fob for a luxury car. "Look, Joe gave me this. Can you believe he gave me a car?"

"He and your brother were close. Joe thinks of you like a niece."

"I know. It's sweet. See you, Tanner."

Gina walked out. As soon as the door closed, Red peeked over the bar.

"She's gone?"

"What was that about?" Ivanov asked. "I thought you

and Gina were dating?"

Red grew sullen. "I caught her cheating on me, but I haven't talked to her about it yet."

"Oh," Ivanov said, while sharing a look with Tanner. Both men knew that a boy like Red could never keep a girl like Gina.

"I saw them kissing in front of a club as I sat in traffic last night. I was driving my mom's car, not the limo, so Gina didn't notice me."

"Did you know the guy she was with?" Ivanov asked, as he leafed through a ledger.

"No, maybe you know him. I got it on my phone… and I can't stop looking at it. I really thought she liked me."

Red showed Ivanov a video of Gina kissing a man on the street, beneath a green neon sign. The man was about her age and handsome.

"I've never seen him before," Ivanov said.

Red placed the phone on the bar and sighed.

Right before the video ended, Tanner glanced at it. He was holding the phone an instant later.

"Play that again, Red."

"You know the guy, Mr. Tanner?"

"Just do it."

Red said, "Yes sir," and brought the video up again.

"What's wrong, Tanner?" Ivanov said.

Tanner stared at the phone, and yeah, he knew the man in the video. It was Liam Murphy.

Gina ran up to the first car in a line of three that were parked inside a building that had once been a paint store.

The front area was empty and waiting for a new tenant to come along. In the rear, on the concrete floor of the storeroom were parked three bland cars that wouldn't attract anyone's attention. However, under each hood was a powerful engine. The men in the warehouse had driven the cars up a ramp at the loading dock before sending in their spy. Liam Murphy was leaning back against the first car with over a dozen men around him.

"Are they both in there?"

Gina kissed him, then spoke. "Joe Pullo is up in his office, but Tanner is sitting at the bar on the left, near the stage."

"Who else is in there?"

"I saw the one they call Bosco, and that Mexican man, Rico, oh, and the manager and some kitchen workers are there too."

Liam smiled. "That's it?"

"Yeah, Sammy Giacconi is out of town."

"Hear that, boys? It's our sixteen to their four and some civilians. This shit won't take a minute."

Gina smiled as she held up the key fob she had shown Tanner. "Look, Pullo gave me a car I could use. Do you believe that? That's how clueless he is."

Liam smiled. "What did you have to do to earn that, crawl under his desk?"

Gina laughed. "He doesn't think of me that way. He thinks I'm still the girl he knew when I lived here."

"Another old-school fucker, just like my father, but his day ends today. Listen up, boys! It's time to lock and load, and remember, that asshole Tanner is mine."

Gina kissed Liam as she pressed herself against him. "Go get this city for me."

Liam winked. "We'll rule the bitch mother like a king and a queen."

19

CHIRP! CHIRP!

Joe watched the video of Gina Rossetti kissing Liam Murphy and felt like throwing Red's phone across the room. Tanner, Ivanov, and Red were in Joe's office along with Bosco and Rico.

"The bastard is using her," Joe said.

"Maybe," Tanner said, "But she was using Red."

Joe looked up from the phone. "What do you mean by that?"

"Gina was seeing Red in secret. I think she was pumping him for information, so that she could pass it on to Liam Murphy."

Joe looked over at Red, and the kid seemed close to tears.

"You and Gina were dating?"

"Kissing, only kissing, Mr. Pullo. She wouldn't let me, I mean… we only kissed."

Tanner clamped a hand on Red's shoulder and spun him around to face him. "Did she know that I would be driving the white van the other night?"

Red had trouble getting the words out as Tanner

pinned him with a stare, but he managed a stuttering reply. "I... I, yes, we talked about things, and I, I mean, she's okay, right? She's like one of us?"

Tanner released Red and pointed down at the club. "Liam Murphy could come through that door at any moment with a small army. Thanks to Gina, he knows how many of us are here."

Joe looked back down at the phone. The video was playing on a repeating loop. The short film was proof that Johnny Rossetti's sister was involved with Moss Murphy's son.

"They must have met in college. They both went to school in California."

Rico took out a cell phone from his pocket. "I can have my crew here in no time."

Joe tossed Red's phone back at him, and the kid fumbled it.

Tanner was thinking things through as Rico talked to one of his men and told him to call others and rush to the club. When Tanner spotted a sales brochure laying beneath a key fob that matched the one Gina had shown him, he plucked it from the desk and held it up.

"Joe, is this for Gina's car?"

"Yeah."

"I have an idea."

SAMMY ARRIVED IN NEW ORLEANS. HE WAS SURPRISED BY how much warmer the weather was there than it had been in New York City. He picked up a car in the airport parking lot that had been left for him by members of the New Orleans mob. It was not a favor, but an arrangement that cost money. The vehicle came with a silenced gun that had been stored away in the trunk. The gun and the car were untraceable.

If Sammy needed to do so, he could abandon the car, if not, he would return it to the airport.

He was wearing a set of gloves, to not leave fingerprints. The gloves were translucent and thin, allowing the wearer to maintain their dexterity. They were almost invisible, as the wearer's skin tone could be seen beneath them.

Using a throwaway phone, Sammy called the old woman who had snitched on Ricky Valente. The woman answered on the third ring in a tone that gave away her wariness.

"Hello?"

"I'm calling to confirm that the man from New York City is still your neighbor."

"What? Oh, wait, I know what you mean. Yeah, he's still here."

"You're certain?"

"Absolutely."

"Good, you'll be contacted again soon."

"And the money?"

"You'll get paid."

"Finally, some good luck."

Sammy ended the call. Snitches were helpful from time to time. That didn't mean he had to like them. The next thing you knew, they'd be snitching on you.

Before leaving the airport, Sammy input the address of the trailer park into the car's GPS. Ricky was living in a nearby community named Metairie. Once Sammy had the directions for the short trip, he placed the car in gear and headed for I-10, determined to make the day Ricky Valente's last.

Miles away, Victor Fenner winced as the lock he was picking opened with an audible click. The lock was on the door of Ricky Valente's rented motor home. Ricky was asleep in a recliner, after having dozed off while watching sports and drinking beer.

Fenner crept inside and closed the door behind him, but he kept a gun pointed at Ricky. A pair of shoes hung by their laces around Fenner's neck. While on Fenner's feet were women's sneakers, unlaced, so that Fenner could squeeze into them. The sneakers were white and clean, but they would soon be soiled by blood.

Ricky slept on. He was oblivious of Fenner's presence, and as he dreamt, Ricky dreamed of being free on a South American beach, while surrounded by hordes of beautiful women.

All in all, it wasn't a bad way to die.

Back in Manhattan, Liam Murphy strutted in front of his men like a general addressing troops. The men were all muscular and many looked as cocky as Liam. Each man wore a bulletproof vest and had a handgun in a hip holster.

Their main weapons, consisting of shotguns and rifles, were in the cars they would use, along with a ski mask for each of them. Their young eyes were filled with a lust for violence and their pockets bulged with ammo.

"Listen up! We're going to make history today by pulling some bold shit. These old-school Mafia assholes have gotten lazy and fat. Unless somebody with some balls takes over, the street gangs will roll over us and we'll have nothing. I ain't going to let that happen. Uh-uh, I'm keeping what I got. But I want more, hell yeah, a shitload more, and we're all gonna run this whole damn country before I get through. Are you with me?"

There was a unanimous shout of agreement.

Liam punched the air with a fist. "We kill everything in sight, but remember, that fucker Tanner is mine."

Gina grabbed Liam and kissed him for luck. In return, he patted her on the ass.

"Get going and I'll meet you back at my apartment."

"Be careful."

Liam laughed. "Baby, I'm the future. You don't ever have to worry about me."

One of the men was pulling hand over hand on the chain that would manually raise the loading dock door on the left side of the building, as the others opened the doors of their vehicles to climb in. When a car alarm sounded from the rear of the building, everyone turned to look that way.

"That's my car," Gina said. "Is someone breaking into my car?"

The alarm stopped abruptly, to be followed by something that sounded like, *Chirp! Chirp!* Next, they could hear an engine start up.

"Someone is stealing my car!"

Liam drew the gun from his holster and strode toward the metal door at the rear of the building. "Somebody's got bad timing."

The men who had been ready to get in the cars drifted behind Liam, thinking they would see a show as their boss shot a would-be car thief. When they filed through the door in the rear, they were disappointed, because no one was in Gina's car.

Gina pressed a button on her key fob and the engine cut off. "Damn. The automatic start must be defective."

Chirp! Chirp!

The vehicle's brake lights flashed, followed by the car starting again.

Gina stamped her foot. "What the hell! It's a new car."

Gina hit the button again, and again the engine cut off.

Liam waved a hand at the car. "You'll get it fixed in Boston, right now, we got a city to take."

The men returned inside and walked toward the cars. The first man who saw Tanner standing in the open doorway of the loading dock bay came to a dead stop, causing the man behind to bump into him.

"Shit," the first man said.

Tanner was holding one of their rifles and pointing it at the group. As several of the men reached for the guns on their hips, they heard shotguns racking. Joe Pullo and Bosco were on their left side, with shotguns propped up on a short concrete block wall that separated the warehouse section from the restrooms. To the right, Rico Nazario and Tamir Ivanov knelt at the rear of a similar wall, behind which, lay an office area. The men were caught in a crossfire with Tanner at their front. The bulletproof vests they wore would do nothing against shotgun blasts to the face.

Liam was the last one inside, after leaving Gina at her car. He had failed to see Tanner, as the bodies of his men blocked his view, nor had he noticed that his men had stopped walking. After locking the back door by sliding a metal bolt in place, Liam turned and was dismayed by what he saw.

"Why are you all just standing around?"

"Because they want to stay alive," Tanner said.

Liam had reached his men. He leaned around them to

look at Tanner. When Joe cleared his throat, Liam jumped, as his head jerked left. After seeing Pullo with a shotgun, one of his *own* shotguns, pointed at his face, Liam hung his head, then peeked to his right and saw Rico and Ivanov.

"Don't be stupid, Liam," Joe said. "Or we'll kill every one of you."

Liam raised his head, sighed, then laughed, as he moved toward Tanner. "The thing with Gina's car, that was you bastards?"

"There's an App that helps you locate your vehicle if you forget where you parked it. I'd say it was worth every penny Joe paid for it," Tanner said.

Liam laughed again, took a deep breath, and dived into a car whose passenger-side door was sitting open. One of his men moved to join him, but he had the back of his head blown apart by a blast from Rico's shotgun. Meanwhile, Liam's other men kept shouting, "Don't shoot! Don't shoot!" with their hands thrust in the air.

The engine of Liam's car roared to life as Tanner sent a shot into the windshield. "You won't make it out of the loading dock, Liam."

The front tires were blown to pieces as Liam put the car in gear. Bosco blew out a rear tire of Liam's car, as Ivanov did the same to the other rear tire. A horrible squelching sound came as Liam turned the steering wheel, and the car lurched backwards, while drifting to the right. Despite riding on two rims, the vehicle's powerful engine caused the damaged car to pick up speed.

Joe sent a blast into the side of the car as it went by him in reverse, while headed for the front of the building. Shotgun pellets blew out the side window and punctured the door, but none of them hit Liam, who was down low and mashing a hand onto the gas pedal.

The car smashed into the wall that separated the

warehouse from the front counter area, plowing through the gypsum panel and aluminum frame while bucking and bouncing. It kept on going, and even picked up speed, as it blasted through the glass display window at the front and smashed into a parked car.

Liam was out of the wreck in a flash, gun in hand, and headed toward the nearest car in a line of vehicles that were stopped at a traffic light. The gray-haired woman inside was gawking at Liam, as was everyone in sight. Liam sent a shot through the window. It missed the woman, but shattered the glass, and Liam unlocked the door.

In her fright, the older woman had taken her foot off the brake, and her car bumped the one in front of it. Liam yanked her out of the car by the hair and got behind the wheel. The cars in front sped off as the light changed, and Liam followed them, but at the first cross street he headed left.

TANNER STOOD INSIDE THE RUINED DISPLAY WINDOW OF THE defunct paint store and watched the car drive out of sight. The rifle he held was powerful, too powerful to risk taking shots at a fleeing car in a crowded city. Even if he'd hit Liam, the round might have kept going and killed someone else.

Tanner went back inside the warehouse, where Liam's soldiers were all looking rather worried. Joe had ordered them to drop their weapons on the ground and back up against a wall. They were fifteen in all, counting the dead man on the floor, and not one of them was older than twenty-two.

"Whatever we do with these guys, we'd better do it soon," Tanner said. "The cops will be here any minute."

Bosco laughed at them. "Any of you punks ever see those pictures of the St. Valentine Day's Massacre? The Tommy guns they used really made a mess of those guys."

One of the men gasped, while another shut his eyes and mouthed a prayer.

Pullo was looking at them with murderous intent as he spoke to Rico. "Lay your shotgun down there beside the guns, Rico, but wipe your prints off first."

Rico raised an eyebrow as he pondered the reason for the order, but he did as Joe said.

Afterward, Joe spoke to the Irish thugs. "Any of you dumb enough to be carrying a wallet on a hit?"

As it turned out, they all had wallets. They held them out to Joe.

"Toss them on the floor by the shotgun."

Although a few of the men hesitated, the last wallet hit the floor as the sound of a siren wailed in the distance.

Pullo pointed toward the wall the car had backed through. "Get the fuck out of here."

The men looked at their wallets lying beside the shotgun with the expended shell, then, over at their dead companion, who'd been killed by the weapon. They would have a hard time explaining away their involvement in the man's death.

"Go! Get the hell out of here before I change my mind and kill all of you," Pullo said.

The men ran toward the gap in the wall. When the last one was out of sight, Tanner, Joe, and the others headed for the back door.

They had left Red with the limo. It was parked around the corner at a hydrant. The limo was there, along with another car. It was the car driven by Gina Rossetti. The limo showed signs of damage to its rear, but the car had fared worse and its airbags had deployed.

They piled into the limo where Gina sat in the back with Red, who was holding a gun on her. The gun was kept in a hidden compartment for emergencies.

Gina had decided to bluff her way out of things. She smiled, as if confused. "Joe, what's going on?"

Pullo ignored her and talked to Red as he took the gun from the boy's hand. The safety was still on.

"Drive us back to the club, Red."

"Yes sir."

"Don't trust him, Uncle Joe. Did you see what he did to my car?"

Joe backhanded Gina across the face with enough force to knock her off the seat. It was the "Uncle" part of her sentence that infuriated him. He had treated the girl like a favored niece, and she had done nothing but betray him. After that, Gina stayed quiet, while giving venomous stares from where she'd landed on the floor of the limo. Tanner noticed that she never shed a tear or asked about the fate of her lover, Liam. Gina Rossetti was one cold bitch.

"I'm going to Boston to kill Moss Murphy," Tanner told Joe. "Do you have any objections?"

"No, but he is a boss. I can't order the hit, not without an approval from the commission in Chicago."

"Murphy doesn't seem to have a problem sending his son after you, commission or no commission."

"That's on him, not me. When this is over, I'll make the commission see that we weren't the ones who broke the peace."

"This won't be a hit, then. It will just be me getting payback for the attack of the other night."

"The kid will warn his father, Tanner. Moss will have enough men at that compound of his to hold off an army."

"I know, and I've planned for that."

"How?"

"A bit of razzle dazzle."

They arrived back at the club to find several men there who all looked relieved to see Joe exit the limo in one piece. After placing Gina up in his office with Bosco to watch over her, Joe joined Tanner down by the bar. Ivanov walked over and spoke to Pullo.

"Joe, I passed the word among the girls and the staff that they had the night off."

"Thanks, Fed, and thanks for your help. I didn't expect that."

Ivanov smiled wryly. "We both know I can no longer claim to have clean hands; I might as well dirty them a little more for a good cause."

Joe looked over at Red. "Are you gonna keep your mouth shut from now on when you talk to women?"

"Yes sir, and I'm sorry."

Joe shook his head in disgust. "I can't really blame you, Andre. You thought she was solid… and so did I."

More men poured into the club, as the word went out that a war was starting. Rico greeted them and gave out instructions.

"It looks like you're going to have your own army here to protect you," Tanner said.

"I'll be fine. Moss Murphy doesn't know anyone like you."

"No, but be careful anyway. He does have Finn Kelly."

"I can handle Kelly, but my guess is that he'll be guarding Murphy."

Tanner looked at his watch. "I'll make it back by morning. Hold down the fort."

Joe offered his hand. "Make sure you come back; we've still got some catching up to do."

Tanner gripped Joe's hand. "And new hell to raise."

20
I OWN YOU!

Fenner held a Smith & Wesson model 41 pistol an inch away from the right temple of Ricky Valente and pulled the trigger.

The dozing Ricky left the land of the living, but he looked little changed from his animate self. The .22 slug that entered his brain lacked the kinetic energy to exit it. Other than a streak of blood down the right side of his face, Ricky looked as if he were sleeping.

Blood dripped onto the carpet and the tops of the white sneakers. Fenner made a point of stepping in it, then he tracked bloody prints across the carpet.

Fenner left the trailer, but only after peeking out to see that no one was around. The nearest trailer other than Julie Ryan's was over fifty yards away. The sound of the target pistol might have been overheard, but Fenner doubted the muted sound would be recognized for what it was.

He left the door to Ricky's trailer open as he headed over to pick the lock on Julie's. Fenner never noticed the strand of hair that fell when he opened the door.

Julie's dog was standing just inside the trailer and growling up at him. Fenner reared back a foot and connected with a kick that sent the dog flying to the other side of the room. Missy landed upside down against a wall, then bolted away, to squeeze beneath the sofa.

Once inside Julie's trailer, Fenner eased his feet out of the sneakers. After looking around, he tucked the incriminating footwear away under the bed. With the gun, he was more creative and took the time to pry off a piece of faux wood paneling, which he slipped the gun behind.

As he walked back out of the trailer, the metal steps felt rough and gritty beneath his stocking feet. Fenner sat on one of those steps and used his hands to brush off the bottom of his socks, so he could put on the shoes dangling around his neck.

After looking about to make certain that no one had come near to investigate the sound of the shot, Fenner headed back to his car. Had anyone gotten nosy, Julie would have been framed for another murder. He still carried a knife and would have used it with skill and experience.

There was a narrow trail through the sparse trees that led to a gap in the bushes. Fenner walked along it and was back on the highway. Less than a hundred yards away was the parking lot of a strip mall. Fenner had parked there instead of the nearer supermarket lot, because the strip mall had a damaged camera at the rear where he could come and go from his vehicle without being captured on video.

Fenner was smiling as he merged back onto the highway. Julie Ryan would have no choice but to do as he wished from this point forward. Soon, the police would be looking for her as a suspect in a murder investigation.

Julie would have a decision to make. Face further

disgrace and incarceration or acquiesce to Fenner's demands and become a slave to him. Slavery was the better choice by far, Fenner believed. Julie would have to service him sexually, yes, but she would also be placed in a comfortable home and have her needs seen to as well. She would never have to cook or clean, as Fenner had servants for that. And while he would demand sex, it would be at infrequent intervals and require nothing perverted.

Fenner made a small laughing sound in his throat as he recalled his past slaves. It always seemed more onerous for them to submit to his demand to be called Master than it was for them to drop to their knees and please him. And yet, call him Master they did, right up until the day he grew tired of them.

He wondered how long Julie Ryan would last before he killed her. He hoped it would be quite some time. And oh, how he couldn't wait to hear her utter the words, "Yes, Master."

Fenner motored along, happy in his insanity.

In New York City, Sara watched as Kevin Kincaid drove his car into the student parking garage. Minutes later, Kevin exited the garage on foot and headed off to class inside a nearby building.

Once again, Sara considered confronting Kevin, but then decided to follow him around for at least two more days. As she watched the young man, she remembered the boy Kevin once was. He had been a cheerful kid before he and Alicia had suffered the loss of their parents. After that, Kevin's nature grew serious and he tended to be withdrawn.

Sara looked at the clock on her car's dashboard and

saw that she had several hours to fill before Kevin would be done with classes for the day. She decided to use the time to visit the lake property and stock the trailer with food for their next visit. What Sara didn't know was that Kevin planned to slip off campus by foot and meet up with the other members of his support group.

Today was to be the day they would rob their last bank and give Ian Seagate a small measure of revenge. However, there was a new player in their game. His name was Luis Zade. Zade had his own ideas about revenge.

Sara drove toward Connecticut. Half an hour later, Kevin Kincaid left campus to go rob a bank.

JULIE WAS APPROACHING HER CAR AFTER LEAVING THE homeless shelter where she volunteered. She was in high spirits. One of the children, an adventurous boy, had fallen off the two-story roof and broken his leg. Julie, a former ER nurse, had cared for him and soothed him until the ambulance arrived. It was the most nursing she had done in a long time; it made her realize how much she missed being a nurse.

She was thinking about that when the man who had ruined her career fell in step beside her.

"I own you, Julie Ryan."

Julie startled at Fenner's appearance and backed away from the madman.

"Get away from me, you freak, or I'll start screaming."

"Your trailer trash boyfriend is dead. I killed him and framed you for his murder."

Julie gawked at Fenner. "What?"

"The man who lives in the trailer next to yours. The one you've been having sex with. I've just come from shooting him. The police will think you've done it. I've made sure of that."

Julie's hands flew to her mouth, as she tried to comprehend the enormity of what Fenner was saying. But it couldn't be true. Shane dead? And herself, framed once again, but for murder?

"No. You're lying. You sick son of a bitch, you're lying!"

Fenner smiled as if he had just heard the wittiest joke. "Go see for yourself. Go on, and once you do, know this—I'm your only way out. Give yourself to me, Julie. I'll keep you safe from the law. Deny me, and you'll never know peace or safety."

"A lie. What you said about Shane is a lie," Julie said, but the words lacked any semblance of conviction. While sobbing, she unlocked her car and climbed inside. When she looked back at Fenner, he was waving at her. She lowered the window and screamed at him. "Who are you? Who the hell are you?"

Fenner's happy smile returned. "Why Julie, I'm your master. Don't you see that by now?"

Julie wiped her tears away and started the car. She was headed to the trailer park. Every bit of her dreaded what she would find.

21
DO ME A FAVOR AND SHOOT ME

As Tanner drove toward Boston he was reminded how negligent he had been in one area of his training.

Being a Tanner required continual striving, constant improvement, and the expanse of knowledge. He was skilled in many martial arts, could converse in over a dozen languages, picked most locks with ease, and was even a competent sailor. Where he had been lax was in acquiring the skills of a pilot.

The four hour driving time between Boston and New York City highlighted how limited his mobility was. He could drive just about anything, but he could fly nothing more than a paper airplane. He would need to correct that weakness.

Duke had provided the flatbed truck he was driving, along with the forged Motor Vehicle and D.O.T. documents. He never thought the man had a sense of humor, but the logos Duke put on the truck doors had changed Tanner's opinion on that subject.

AAA Exterminators – No Job Is Too Big – Phone 555-482-6637

The 555 area-code held no meaning, but the phone number, 482-6637 spelled out I Tanner.

Why an exterminator would need to own a flatbed truck was a mystery to Tanner, but he doubted anyone would give the bland vehicle a second look.

Tanner checked his watch and saw that he should have plenty of time to prepare for his attack on Moss Murphy's estate. Although, outlandish and theatrical, Tanner didn't doubt that his UFO ruse would work. He knew human nature and understood the innate curiosity that all possessed. The thugs protecting Murphy would drop their guard as they stared in wonder at the prop crated on the truck, and like moths drawn to a flame, they would burn.

JULIE PARKED HER CAR, LEFT IT RUNNING, AND RUSHED UP the stairs leading to Ricky Valente's trailer. She stopped in the doorway when she saw the bloody sneaker prints on the carpet, then sighed with relief as her eyes fell on Ricky.

Asleep, Julie thought, *Shane is only sleeping.*

She was in denial. Despite her medical training, her experience, and the evidence gathered by her senses, Julie did not want to believe that she was being framed again, and for such a terrible act as the taking of an innocent life.

Shane had been her friend. He had nothing to do with the maniac hounding her. If he were dead, his death would be on her conscience, even though she had done nothing personally to cause his demise.

So she told herself that the malodorous odor throughout the trailer wasn't caused by the vacated bowels of a fresh corpse. And the darkening red marks on the carpet? Well, they were just part of a sick joke.

"Shane, Shane wake up! That man I was telling you about is here."

Julie had been walking toward the body as she spoke. When she was less than a yard away she could no longer deny the awful truth. The man she knew as Shane was dead, as dead as anyone will ever be, and the bloodstains marring the carpet were real.

Julie tripped and came close to falling as she spun to head back out the door. She was crying again, her mind roiled in turmoil. She jumped back in her car, wanting to get away, to run, to hide once more.

"Missy?"

She had to get her dog. Julie had placed a hair between the door and the jamb every time she left to go out. The hair was no longer there, but Julie didn't even notice, because when she placed her key in the lock she realized it wasn't needed.

There was a red spot right inside the door that stained the cheap beige carpet. It was blood.

"Missy? Baby, where are you?"

A small brown head poked out from under the sofa. Julie walked over and scooped the dog up in her arms, as she checked the hound for injuries. Missy appeared to be fine, and yet, she had never hidden under the sofa before.

Julie damned Fenner's soul without even knowing his name. Poor Missy had been abused as a puppy. It was beyond cruel for her to suffer again. At least the dog was alive, which was more than Shane could claim. Julie wiped at tears again. She didn't stop to pack anything, she only wanted to get away.

When she stepped outside, Fenner was there, pointing up at the sky.

"Hear that, Julie? Those are sirens. I called the police.

You see, there really is no choice. Submit to me, serve me, and you'll be spared being locked up again."

Julie stood there dumbly, as the sound of the sirens grew closer.

Fenner held up a key ring. "You might have noticed that your car has stopped running. That's because I have your keys." He made a casual gesture and sent the keys off into the brush, then grinned. "I own you, Julie Ryan. Come with me and stay out of prison."

Fenner smiled. He couldn't help it. This is where he always got them. They all told themselves that they would just humor him long enough to get away, to have time to think, maybe even take control of the situation and force Victor Fenner to admit his guilt to the authorities. But what they were doing was stepping upon the slipperiest of slopes.

When it was safe again, they all left him, but not before he made certain they could contact him. Later, as the police grew closer, or they were refused assistance by family and friends, then, they would seek him out.

Who wouldn't refuse them aid or shelter, when all they offered as assurance of their innocence was a tale of an unnamed bogeyman. At this stage, the making of a slave was fraught with difficulties.

Over the years, several of the women had been apprehended before he could save them. Once, he'd even lost one to suicide. That one still bruised him, she had been an especially beautiful redhead and would have been an enjoyable slave. Of the ones that had been arrested, all of them were serving time, and there was a special case of a failed slave being committed to a mental institution.

Fenner was confident that Julie would step upon that slippery slope and begin the final process, but to his surprise, she bolted toward the highway with the dog in her arms.

He sighed. For as much trouble as she was, she had better be worth it, or her stint as a slave would be brief. Fenner followed Julie's path as he headed to his car, knowing he could find her again as she scurried along the highway.

Sammy wondered what was going on, as two police cars turned into the entrance of the trailer park he'd been headed to. Were the cops there because of some reason that concerned Ricky Valente, or on another matter?

Sammy drove by the entrance and parked on the side of the road. He had been there for only seconds when a blonde emerged from the bushes. She was beautiful, full of curves, and crying her eyes out. In her arms was a little brown dog. The blonde rushed along the highway while looking behind her, as if she were being chased. Sammy saw no such pursuit, but playing a hunch, he moved along and caught up to her.

"Hi, are you all right? You seem upset."

The woman was about to answer when movement to her left took her attention away from him. Sammy looked out the back window and saw a man in a blue suit exiting from the same spot the woman had.

"No," she whispered.

"Are you afraid of that man? Hop in and I'll take you away from him."

The woman hesitated, but when the man ran toward her, she ripped open the car door and practically dived onto the bench seat.

"Go! He's coming, oh please just drive."

Sammy did as she suggested, leaving the man behind on the highway.

~

FENNER WAS FURIOUS. HE HAD NOT EXPECTED JULIE TO BE offered a ride so quickly. He ran for his car. He had left it in the same parking lot as before, but he estimated that Julie was several miles ahead by the time he merged onto the roadway.

He had an advantage, in that he knew what their vehicle looked like, but they had no idea what he was driving. A second blessing was the traffic on I-10. It was moving slow. If Julie's rescuer decided to head onto the highway, Fenner would have a good chance of catching sight of them by weaving through gaps in the traffic.

Fenner grew calm by telling himself that the good Samaritan who had picked Julie up on the highway was a minor inconvenience. Better yet, Fenner would turn the man into an asset. He would kill the man with the knife he carried and leave the body in the car. Video from the traffic cameras near the homicide would be scrutinized and evidence of Julie riding with the man would come to light.

With two counts of murder hanging over her head, Julie Ryan would beg Fenner to take her in. All in all, the Samaritan's arrival could be a good thing, but first, Fenner had to catch up to them.

~

SAMMY TOOK A LEFT OFF VETERANS MEMORIAL Boulevard and turned onto Cleary Avenue in Metairie, Louisiana. The blonde sitting in his passenger seat said her name was Julie and that the man chasing after her had just framed her for the murder of a friend.

"What's the friend's name?" Sammy said.

"Shane Ryder."

"And you say you were friends?"

"More like friendly."

Sammy looked her over and could see why Ricky would want to get friendly with her. Apparently, Julie understood what he was thinking, because she shook her head.

"We weren't lovers and I had no reason to hurt him. I liked Shane."

Sammy passed a field that had a baseball diamond and pulled into the parking lot of a church. Except for his vehicle, the lot was empty. After cutting off the engine, he turned in his seat to face Julie.

"This Shane Ryder, was he a big guy with curly brown hair?"

"He was big, and I'm sure he dyed his hair blond. How did you know that?"

"His real name was Ricky Valente. I've been looking for Ricky for weeks."

Julie gave Sammy a wary look. "Shane told me just last night that he was on the run from someone. I guess that was you."

Sammy took out his gun. Julie stared at him as if he had just done a magic trick. The weapon had a sound suppressor attached and was made of blued steel, to prevent rust. It looked as deadly as it was.

"Where's the money, Julie?"

"What money?"

"Ricky stole money from the organization I'm a part of. Did you kill him for it?"

"No!"

Julie's vehement reply was so charged with anger that Sammy was tempted to believe her, but he had met good liars before.

"Tell me where the money is, and I'll let you go. Get greedy and stupid, try to bluff me and say you know nothing, and I'll hand you over to the cops for Ricky's murder."

Julie opened her mouth, then shut it. After giving her head a little shake, she sat Missy down between her feet and pointed at a spot on her chest where her heart was located.

"Shoot me, you son of a bitch! First that maniac threatens me and now you. Shoot me and put me out of my misery. You'd be doing me a favor."

Sammy gazed into Julie's blue eyes for several seconds, then holstered his gun.

"This man who framed you, did he know that Ricky had money hidden away somewhere?"

"I don't know. I don't even know who he is. Don't you understand? This man, he's like some sort of stalker, only he hides his tracks well. He deliberately ruined my life by framing me for stealing drugs from the hospital I worked at."

"You're a doctor?"

"I was an ER nurse, and a damn good one."

Sammy hung his head. "Is Ricky's body in his trailer?"

Julie nodded, as her last view of the man she knew as Shane Ryder came to mind.

"Damn!"

"What?" Julie said.

"I know Ricky. He'd keep that money close, like right inside the trailer. That means the cops have it."

"Money? The hell with your money. I'm going to go to

prison for killing Shane and I have no way to prove my innocence."

The next words out of Sammy's mouth surprised him as much as they shocked Julie.

"I'll help you clear your name."

"How? And who are you?"

"I'm Sammy."

"Hello Sammy, my name is Julie Ryan and my life has gone to shit."

Sammy sighed. "Welcome to the club."

22

MAKE A WITHDRAWAL WITHOUT ALL THAT MESSY PAPERWORK

Professor Ian Seagate smiled as he watched a small band of bicycle messengers descend on the city block where he was about to rob a bank.

He and his "crew" were dressed as bicycle messengers and wore helmets, mirrored sunglasses, and backpacks. They had trained for weeks and each of them had a route of escape where a change of clothes awaited them.

As Sara had noticed, the bright orange overlay on their helmets could be removed and reveal the more common white beneath it. They would do that as they left the bank and blend in with all the other bike messengers.

Seagate would rob the bank with Kevin and Roland, while Gabriel would be watching the man they hoped to frame, and Juan Vega made calls to bicycle delivery services around the city. There should be a score of other bicycle messengers in the area when they left the bank.

Any cops arriving on the scene and getting the word that the bank robbers were dressed like messengers would be faced with a difficult task. They would have to try to apprehend over a dozen possible suspects, all of whom would be moving swiftly away from the scene.

"Three more guys just showed up, Professor," Kevin Kincaid said. He was astride a bike and in the middle between Seagate and the nervous Roland, who fidgeted on his bike seat as if it were too hot to sit on.

Seagate sent off a text to Gabriel, who was parked outside the motel room of the man they were about to frame. Gabriel texted him back, telling him that the man was still alone in the room, and that he had heard loud snoring when he'd last walked past the man's door. Seagate grinned. He was finally going to get his revenge, and how sweet it would be.

"All right guys, just like before, we get in, get the money, and get out."

Kevin and Roland nodded, then they casually biked down to the bank on the corner. The nervous Roland stayed with the bikes and was a lookout for trouble, while Seagate and Kevin went inside.

They had done this four times before while wearing other disguises, such as the Santa Claus suits worn during their last robbery. They were confident, but not only because they had experience, they had also researched their targets well.

The tellers at this branch were behind a simple counter with no bars. No sliding panels would drop from the ceiling and the doors wouldn't lock to keep them inside. They would be in the bank for less than a minute, just enough time to be handed cash by a teller.

Unlike most bank robbers, they didn't care about the money. Their only goal was the act itself. Bank robbery was the whole point. It was a felony and a federal crime that carried stiff penalties. It was an ideal crime to frame their targets with.

The prison sentence was the same for a thousand-dollar bank robbery as it was for a hundred-thousand-dollar bank robbery. The money meant nothing.

Seagate and Kevin saw an angry bike messenger as they got off their bikes. The man had likely learned that the call to get him to the area was a phony one. He wouldn't be the last.

Once inside the bank, Seagate bypassed the line of customers and strode over to the end of the counter where a female teller was counting a bundle of cash. After pointing his fake, yet realistic-looking gun at her, Seagate smiled. "I'll take that money off your hands, and you don't have to bother with the paperwork."

In Louisiana, Julie Ryan told Sammy more about her life and how a madman destroyed it, so she would have no choice but to give in to him.

"And you say you don't even know his name?"

"No, and that makes it creepier, because it means he must have been watching me and thinking about me for a long time. I was in jail for months after he framed me the first time. When I was released, he just showed up and admitted what he did."

"You were right when you said he was insane. Only a crazy person would do something like that to you."

Julie groaned. "Six months in county Jail was horrible. I don't even want to imagine what doing years in a prison must be like."

"We need to find this man and pass him over to the cops. Otherwise, you won't have a chance of clearing your name."

Julie made a sour face as she looked around. "In the past, he's always found me."

Sammy took out his gun again and held it loosely. "Let's hope he finds us soon."

Sara was driving back from the lake property when the news came over the radio. Men dressed like bike messengers had just robbed a bank in lower Manhattan. Sara thought about what Tanner had said concerning the items she'd seen in the rear of the van.

It sounds like they're going to dress up like bicycle messengers.

And that's what they did, to rob a bank.

"Oh Kevin," Sara sighed. She understood that Kevin Kincaid was in serious trouble. If caught and convicted, he could serve a decade or more in a federal prison. Sara thought about the quickest route to take to her new destination. She was headed to Professor Seagate's house in Tarrytown, having assumed that Kevin and his friends would meet there after the robbery.

She was right about that, but there would be someone else there as well, a thief and a murderer named Luis Zade, who was planning to rob and kill the group.

Sara drove faster, as intuition told her that Kevin Kincaid faced more trouble than the implications of breaking the law could bring down upon him. No, there was danger as well, she simply knew it.

Sara removed the knife she kept in her purse, opened it, and sat it up in a cup holder. As she slowed to take a curve, she reached over and removed a gun from her glove box. She could be dangerous too.

23
HOP IN!

Fenner tapped a fist against the top of his dashboard in triumph as he spotted Sammy's car in the parking lot of a church. He had slowed when spotting it, but he didn't stop. Instead, he drove on to the next intersection where he made three consecutive right turns to park on the street in front of a small, but well-maintained home.

From where he was, Fenner could see Sammy in profile. The fact that Sammy was young and good-looking didn't please Fenner. Julie might see in the man a chance at a new protector. Fenner needed her in panic mode if she were to give up all hope and submit to him. A stranger like Sammy might renew her confidence in herself.

There was also the outside chance that the stranger might be so beguiled by her beauty that he would offer to give Julie an alibi for the time of the murder. He could claim that he picked her up from her job at the homeless shelter and was with her ever since. If the man were respectable enough, the cops would believe him, and Julie's trailer wouldn't be searched, granting her time to get rid of the evidence.

Fenner couldn't have that. No, he would kill the stranger and place Julie in more legal peril. She would see the power Fenner possessed and how futile any hope of rescue was. She would finally submit and become his slave.

Yes, the stranger had to die. Fenner left his car while holding a knife and moved toward Sammy's open window. One flash of the sharp blade and the stranger's throat would be cut. Fenner made a face of disgust when he thought about the gush of blood that would result. He detested any sort of mess.

After entering the parking lot and moving with stealth, Fenner eased his way over to the driver's side of Sammy's car. While Sammy and Julie were preoccupied by their conversation, Fenner inched closer to Sammy's open window. Once there, he raised the knife, and prepared to strike.

LUIS ZADE WAS SMILING AT THE SURPRISED LOOKS ON THE faces of Juan Vega's friends. They had gawked when Juan entered the barn with Zade, and Juan had been trying to explain the situation ever since.

"I had no choice. He figured out that I framed his brother."

The professor, the one named Seagate, was crimson with anger. "Why did you tell him everything, Juan? You didn't have to tell him about us."

Juan shook his head. "I did. You weren't there. He would have kept hurting me if I didn't tell the truth, he would have hurt me bad."

"Enough talk," Zade said. "Where's the money?"

Everyone looked over at Kevin, the handsome dark-haired kid. He was still wearing a backpack, like a bike messenger would, even though he had changed into his regular clothes, jeans and a sweatshirt.

"How much are you carrying, kid?"

Kevin swallowed once before answering and Zade smiled at his nervousness.

If the boy is scared now, he'll be shitting himself when the shooting starts.

"We don't know how much exactly, but it, it looked like a lot this time." Kevin adjusted a strap on the backpack. "And it's heavy too."

"The heavier the better, walk over here and hand it to me."

Seagate held up a hand. "Hold on a second. We need that money."

"Yeah, Juan told me about that. You want to frame some other poor bastard."

"Poor bastard? That *poor bastard* as you call him killed my fiancée."

"On purpose?"

"No, Emily was shot by accident, but he still murdered her."

"Hey, Seagate, shit happens, and there are other women in the world. But look at you, you took these kids and turned them into frame artists and bank robbers. You're no saint."

"That's not true," Kevin said. "We're all in this together, and we're not kids. We had a plan to get justice and it worked."

Zade smiled. "Kid, if it had worked, we wouldn't be talking. The plan went to shit and now it's time to pay up for fucking with my brother. Hand over the money."

"We need that money," Seagate said. "The bastard that killed Emily… my Emily. He must pay, don't you understand? He must pay!"

"Mr. Zade," Juan said, and Zade turned his head to look at him. "What if we gave you most of the money but kept some to help out the professor?"

Seagate relaxed. "Good thinking, Juan, yes, that would work. We only need a little of the money and the paper bands with the tellers' initials on them."

"Fuck that!" Zade told him. "I want all the money, every last dollar."

"But why?" Seagate whined. "Don't you see how perfect this is? If we used Juan's idea, it would be win-win."

"I have an idea for an even better plan," Zade said.

Seagate spread his arms wide. "Fine, I'm open to suggestions."

Zade reached behind his back and grabbed his gun. "My plan is simple. I win, you lose."

Zade brought up the gun, shot Seagate in the chest, then fired a bullet into Juan Vega's mouth, which had been opened in shock.

As Vega's body fell to the floor and Seagate lay dying, Zade pointed the gun at Kevin. "The backpack—Now!"

Missy yapped at Fenner when he was seconds away from slicing open Sammy's throat. The strident sound startled Fenner enough to make him hesitate, but he recovered and reached inside the car.

Julie screamed, "Don't!" as Fenner grabbed Sammy's hair and yanked his head back, in preparation of getting a clean deep slice across Sammy's throat. With no time to do anything else, Sammy fired three shots over his shoulder, grateful that the gun was silenced, otherwise, he might have deafened his own ear.

Two of the rounds missed, as they went between

Fenner and the car, to ricochet off the ground. But Fenner released Sammy as the third shot struck the side of his right knee. Julie's dog, Missy, jumped out the open passenger window and sped away. Fenner's actions, along with the sound of the shots, even muffled as they were, had disturbed the sensitive dog.

When Julie opened the car door to chase after Missy, Sammy grabbed for her arm, but he was too late to stop her from going after Missy.

Lying on the ground, Fenner saw her retreating feet and shouted her name. "Julie!"

Sammy stepped out of the car as Fenner was getting up by holding onto the rear door handle. Fenner's crazed face told Sammy that Julie had told him the truth. The man was mad.

"She's mine!" Fenner said, while taking a swipe at Sammy with the knife. The movement caused Fenner to grit his teeth from the pain of his wound. He fell back against the car before sliding to the ground.

Sammy shot him in the other knee and Fenner howled in agony as the knife fell from his hand. Fenner was going nowhere on his own, so Sammy got back in his vehicle and went in pursuit of Julie.

He found her out on the avenue. She was leaning over the front of a police car and getting cuffed. To be arrested that quickly meant the police believed she had killed Ricky and had been busy looking for her. Sammy's first impulse was to go to Julie's aid, but he couldn't.

He was carrying an unregistered gun that could be linked to the wounded man in the church parking lot. The only reason he was in Louisiana was to commit murder and retrieve mob money.

Julie being associated with someone named Giacconi could do more harm than good, and the law might possibly believe that she had taken a contract to kill Ricky for the Giacconis.

Sammy drove back the way he'd come, where Fenner's screams of pain were gaining the attention of the nearby homeowners, some of whom were standing on their porches and looking around.

Fenner was out of their line of sight where he lay, as he was blocked from their view by a row of hedges. Still, more cops would be called to deal with him as well.

Minutes later, Sammy abandoned the car in a mall parking lot after wiping it down. Ricky was dead, the money was lost, and now, Sammy had become involved in a separate mess.

He had no idea how he could help Julie Ryan, but he'd be damned if he wouldn't try.

KEVIN WAS BREATHING THROUGH HIS MOUTH IN SHORT shallow breaths. He had never been so scared in his life, not even the first time he robbed a bank. His best friend, Juan, was dead. Dead! And Professor Seagate was bleeding on the floor. The man who had shot them was pointing his gun at him. Kevin knew the man would kill him.

He was taking the backpack off, as Zade had ordered him to do, when the car crashed open the barn doors. Zade was hit on the back of the head by the left section of the doors and knocked to the ground, dazed. The car stopped just inside the barn. For a moment, all Kevin could make out of the driver was a hand clutching a knife. The blade punctured the airbags blocking his view, and a woman appeared. After spotting him, she was gesturing for him to get in the car. It was his sister, Alicia, but no, not Alicia, but Alicia's friend, a woman named Sara Blake.

Sara had been coming up the driveway when she heard the shots fired at Seagate and Juan.

After that, her only thought had been to get Kevin to safety. Without changing her speed, she headed for the barn doors, then braked at the last moment, as she hoped to ram the doors open, but not smash them to pieces. The impact jolted her, as did the deployment of the airbags, yet both had been expected.

After deflating the airbags, Sara looked around. There was a man lying on the floor to her left, with a gun just out of reach of his hand. On the floor beside him was a dead boy who looked as young as Kevin, while a wounded man writhed in agony just a few feet in front of her car.

The man was Professor Seagate. Sara recognized him from his photo on the college's website. Seagate had been shot at least once in the chest. There were two other boys standing near Kevin. One of them had dark hair, while the other was skinny and blond. The blond appeared to have wet himself, as a stain covered the front of his pants.

Sara gestured for Kevin to get in the car. When Kevin didn't move, from either shock or fear, Sara leaned across and opened the passenger door.

"Get in!"

Kevin moved toward her, as did Gabriel and Roland. To her left, Zade sat up and rubbed his temples as he tried to clear his head. Kevin folded down the passenger seat and climbed into the rear, Gabriel followed, and as Roland was getting in, Zade picked up his gun.

Sara fired through the open window and missed hitting Zade by an inch. Zade, realizing he had no cover, rolled behind a barn door, but not before he got off a wild shot that went high. Roland, who was nervous at the best of times, shrieked and bolted outside.

Sara let him go, fired three shots at the wooden door Zade had disappeared behind, and put her car in reverse. Sara was grateful that the car continued to run after her airbag deployed. Had the collision with the barn door caused major damage to the vehicle, her engine might have stopped running, as a safety precaution. If that had happened, she would have had to engage in a firefight inside the barn with Kevin at risk.

Zade reappeared as Sara was turning the car around in a skidding turn to head toward the road. The shots they'd exchanged had all missed, and Sara and the boys drove away.

ZADE LET OUT A SCREAM OF FRUSTRATION AS SARA'S CAR sped around a curve in the gravel driveway, spitting up stones as it went. Everything was a damn mess now that the woman drove off with those boys, and the one named Kevin still had the money. Zade rushed to his car to go in pursuit, but he hesitated after opening the door. Professor Seagate was still alive.

Zade took two steps back toward the barn, but then he returned to the car. No one had heard the shots or the car crashing the doors open. In the shape Seagate was in, he would die before he got help. The important thing was to catch up to the woman and the boys. The woman! Zade had seen her somewhere before. He was certain of it, but where?

Vega! He had seen a picture of the woman on Vega's phone the night before. She was Kevin Kincaid's sister and she owned a flower shop, no, wait, a dance studio. But which dance studio?

Zade rushed back into the barn and checked Juan's body for the phone. After removing it from a back pocket, Zade went through the photos until he found the photo of Juan with Kevin and Alicia. They were standing in front of Alicia's dance studio and smiling.

"Village Dance & Ballet Academy," Zade said, as behind him, Seagate moaned in agony.

Zade glared down at the professor, saw that the man was dying, and laughed.

"Die, fucker! Suffer for framing my brother."

Zade ran from the barn with Juan's phone in his hand and headed for the city.

AT THE SAME MOMENT ZADE WAS TAKING JUAN'S PHONE from his back pocket, Kevin had been ending a call he made anonymously.

"They're sending a cop with the ambulance, Sara. I hope Zade doesn't shoot at them."

"He won't be there. He'll be chasing after us. I only hope your professor survives long enough to receive their help."

Sara rounded a curve in the road and there was Roland. He was running as fast as when he'd left the barn in a mad dash for safety.

Sara slowed until she was even with him, and Kevin called his friend's name. "Roland! It's okay. Hop in."

Roland slowed, stopped, and after a look inside to make certain it was safe to do so, he got in the car.

Sara had the car moving again, as she realized how far Roland had run in a short time.

"You're Roland?"

He answered breathlessly. "Yes."

"Do you run track, Roland?"

"No."

"Consider taking it up. I think you're a natural."

24
A CASE OF MISTAKEN IDENTITY

Tanner arrived in Boston and found a spot near the waterfront where he could park the flatbed.

It was a shipping and receiving area for a plumbing supply company that had closed for the day. The luncheonette on the corner was still open, and Tanner bought a turkey sandwich and an iced tea.

After eating, he sat inside the cab of the truck and went over the satellite images of Moss Murphy's estate one more time. Murphy had the lavish home built when he had designs on fitting in with the upper crust of Boston society. However, the upper crust knew a thug when they saw one, no matter how rich the thug had become.

The wrought iron gates surrounding the home were high, but decorative, the grounds full of rolling hills, not land mines, while the house itself had wide windows without bars. Getting inside the house to kill Murphy would be a thing of ease. Tanner just had to navigate his way past upwards of fifty armed men.

The faux UFO in the crate would help with that, among other surprises Tanner had planned.

When he was satisfied that he had done everything to prepare for his attack on the home. Tanner leaned back and closed his eyes. His plan would work best at night, which was well over an hour away.

He set his watch to wake him in forty-five minutes. A short nap would revitalize him after the long drive and the food. As he was falling asleep, he wondered how Sara's day was turning out. She had told Tanner she was going to follow around a college kid all day, and maybe visit the lake property. That was good. She deserved a quiet day.

WHILE SARA HAD DRIVEN FAST, ZADE HAD DRIVEN FASTER, while also using his phone to get the dance studio's address. He made it to Alicia's studio soon after Sara had. His grin was wide as he spotted her car double-parked with the flashers going, and he pulled in front of her vehicle.

Zade pressed his face against the windows of the dance studio and saw Kevin Kincaid and his sister hugging inside as Gabriel and Roland stood nearby. The backpack with the money in it was on the floor, leaning against a mirror.

Zade bit the inside of his cheek as he prepared to walk inside the studio and murder four people. He couldn't use the gun for anything but intimidation. Not in the city, where a passing cop could hear the shots and arrest him before he could get away. The thing to do was to have them tie each other up, then he could kill them quietly, maybe with a knife, or by strangling them.

Zade stared in at Alicia, still thinking he was looking at Sara, and a thought occurred to him. Alicia was dressed in a red leotard and white ballet slippers. Had the woman firing at him been wearing a leotard? Perhaps it had been concealed by her jacket.

When movement in the glass showed him a woman's reflection, Zade blinked in confusion, as he saw Sara coming up behind him. He then stiffened as he felt Sara press her gun against his left side.

Turning his head to look at her, he asked, "You're a twin?"

"I'm an ex-FBI agent who has killed in and out of the line of duty. If you so much as twitch, I'll put you down."

Zade's eyes moved about in all directions as he sought to come up with a way out. "The dead kid, Juan, he wanted to share the money. We could still do that?"

"No deal."

"Think about it. If we work together your boy in there never does a day in prison."

"He just gets to look over his shoulder for the rest of his life, because sooner or later, you'll come for him."

"Same goes for you, bitch. Either we make a deal or someday I'll find your ass, then you'll be the one put down."

Sara sighed. "I believe you."

Sara removed the gun from Zade's ribs and pointed it downward, while aiming.

She fired, hitting Zade on the inside of his right leg and creating havoc with his femoral artery. As his leg buckled, Zade leaned against the window and grabbed Sara's gun, gripping the weapon's warm barrel as he tried to wrest it away from her. When that failed, he staggered backwards.

As he freed his gun, his legs gave out before he could take aim. He fell sideways against the glass window of the studio once more, before sliding down to the pavement.

Passersby were startled by the shooting and most ducked behind cars, as inside the dance studio, Alicia,

Kevin, Gabriel, and Roland turned toward the window with startled faces.

Sara kicked the gun out of Zade's hand before leaning down toward him. He was sitting in a puddle of his own blood and breathing rapidly.

"I don't take well to threats. Goodbye, Mr. Zade."

Zade raised a hand, but it dropped just as quickly.

A vehicle with government plates braked near the curb. Sara placed her gun on the ground and extended her hands to show that they were empty. When she saw who was in the car, she smiled and lowered her arms. FBI Agent Jake Garner left his vehicle with another agent and rushed to Sara.

"Are you all right?"

"I am, what about Professor Seagate, did he make it?"

Jake shook his head, then asked a question. "Is this one of the bank robbers you called me about?"

"No, and it's a complicated story; there are people inside the dance studio you'll want to talk with."

The agent who'd accompanied Jake had been calling for an ambulance. When the call was done, he checked for a pulse on Zade.

"Shit," the man said. "I should have ordered a meat wagon. He's dead."

"What happened here, Sara?"

"We struggled over my gun and it went off."

"The weapon on the ground over there, that's his?"

"Yes, and you'll find his prints on my gun."

A police car arrived. After Garner explained the situation, the cops took over the scene.

Jake placed a hand on Sara's arm. "It's going to be a long evening of reports and interviews."

"One of the bank robbers is a college student named

Kevin Kincaid. I'll appreciate anything you can do for him."

Garner let out a low whistle through his teeth. "That's easier said than done."

"I know."

∽

HOURS LATER, SARA WATCHED ALICIA KISS HER BROTHER goodbye. Kevin was being transferred from FBI headquarters to the Manhattan Detention Complex, where he would await arraignment on several charges. Sara was facing no charges in the death of Luis Zade. A tourist had snapped a photo of Zade grabbing Sara's gun and gave a statement that the "Big man was harassing the woman before the shooting, by standing very close to her."

Witness testimony can be unreliable. That doesn't make it bad in all cases.

Sara felt as if she had failed Alicia. Her old friend had come to her for help and now her brother would likely serve years in prison.

Alicia walked toward Sara. She had red eyes from crying and was clutching a tissue moist with tears. To Sara's surprise, Alicia gripped her in a fierce hug.

"Thank you, Sara. If not for you my brother would be dead. Kevin said that man Zade was about to shoot him when you appeared."

"You're welcome, Alicia. But I feel horrible that Kevin has to do time."

"He deserves it, despite his motives, and I'm so furious at Professor Seagate for using Kevin the way he did. If that man wasn't already dead, I'd kill him myself."

"What did Agent Garner say about Kevin's chances of

getting a break because of their motives? After all, they never kept the money."

"No, but they used it to frame people. Anyway, Agent Garner said he'll do what he can to help Kevin and the others get in front of the right judge."

"Jake is a good man."

"He's the one Jennifer married, isn't he?"

"Yes."

"He's very handsome, and I appreciate his help. Please pass my gratitude along to him."

"I will."

THEY WALKED OUTSIDE TOGETHER, WHERE ALICIA HAILED A taxi. Sara would have to do so as well. Her car was impounded, as part of the investigation.

Before climbing inside the cab, Alicia thanked Sara again and kissed her on the cheek.

"Are you taking a taxi uptown or is your new man picking you up?"

"I'll be taking a taxi too."

"I want to meet this new guy of yours. Thomas is his name, right?"

"Thomas Myers," Sara said, using Tanner's alias.

"What sort of work does he do?"

"You might say he's a high-level trouble shooter."

"I'm surprised he hasn't come to pick you up, after the trying day you've had."

Sara smiled. "He's in the Boston area, on business."

25

DISTRACT, DEFLECT, DESTROY

The UFO was not much more than a large drone with sophisticated light and sound systems. With the lights off, it made an excellent reconnaissance tool, since it was equipped with a night vision camera and thermal imaging.

While still outside the estate, Tanner took a few minutes to fly the craft over the area to get a look at what he would face. There were perimeter patrols along the fence, both on foot and in vehicles. One of the vehicle patrols was headed his way.

Over two dozen men were outside the home. They were gathered in small groups, with here and there a single man, likely a sniper. Tanner counted four of them. A thermal scan of the home's interior disclosed the presence of more men, perhaps as many as ten. While some of the men outside wore suits, most were dressed in jeans, along with a jacket for the chill in the air. Tanner wore dark-blue slacks, while his reversible jacket was turned to display its gray color. The jacket also held many rounds of spare ammo, and a flash bang grenade.

Tanner brought the modified drone down to rest on a

knoll, grabbed up a sniper rifle with a sound suppressor, then lowered himself to the ground. The perimeter patrol came around a curve in the road. They were creeping along while keeping an eye out for anything unusual. After spotting the flatbed truck, the man in the passenger seat raised a phone up as if to dial. Tanner shot him, then the driver. Their car rolled on, lost speed, although it had been going slow in the first place, and came to rest against a tree.

Tanner ran to the vehicle and maneuvered the dead driver into the back seat. The man in the passenger seat, although dead, was still sitting upright, as he was held in place by his seatbelt. Tanner kicked the shattered windshield out of its frame, backed the car away from the tree, and continued the route the patrol would have taken.

After covering a short distance, Tanner drove the car off the road and parked it next to the wrought-iron fence. He was about to leave the vehicle to climb over the fence when he spotted the tag hanging around his passenger's neck. It was a silver chain, which glittered in the moonlight. When he looked in the rear seat at the driver's body, he saw a similar tag hanging off his belt. They were ID tags, but also more than that. They contained an RFID chip, a Radio-Frequency Identification transponder, like the type used on animals to locate or identify them.

Tanner gave a little laugh. He wasn't the only one using technology. There must be an RFID reader on the property, or perhaps several, and they were being used to distinguish friendlies from the unfriendly.

Tanner took the tag off the passenger and hung it from his neck. If anyone aimed a reader at him, he would register. Once he showed proof of belonging, he wouldn't be questioned, or so he hoped.

Tanner climbed onto the car's roof, then went over the

fence and landed on the other side. He took out the remote that controlled the drone and sent it airborne, where it would hover high above the property in a circling pattern.

Once the drone was up with its camera running, Tanner memorized a route that would help him avoid anyone until he made it to the front of the house. There was always the chance that he'd be spotted by a sniper, but if so, they would identify his tag and disregard him as an enemy.

Upon reaching the area at the side of the huge home, Tanner saw that many of the men were swarthy, while some had face tattoos like the men who'd attack him on the highway. It appeared that Moss Murphy had aligned himself with one of the gangs seeking to move in on what the Italian and Irish mobs had controlled for so long.

Perhaps Liam Murphy had made connections within a Los Angeles gang while going to college in the area. However they had come together, they were united against the Giacconi Family.

As he moved closer to the house, a man looked down at his phone while pointing it his way. The man was looking for an RFID chip. Once the chip was confirmed, the man stepped closer. He had a lazy left eye and was staring at Tanner as if he suspected something was wrong about him, despite the confirmation of an RFID chip.

When he spoke, he revealed a strong Hispanic accent. "You got a cigarette?"

Tanner wondered if the man's question was a code phrase to be answered in a certain way, or if he just wanted a smoke.

"Sorry, no cigarettes."

"How come I don't remember seeing you earlier at the meeting inside the house?"

"I've been out on patrol most of the night," Tanner said, "and I don't remember seeing you either."

Tanner pressed a button on the remote, and the night sky lit up in a blaze of rotating color. It was time to distract.

His wary companion forgot all about him as he gazed up in wonder. Lit up the way it was, the damn thing really did look like the classic idea of a UFO.

Tanner pressed a second button and a humming sound began. It was loud enough that he could feel the vibration on his skin, like a tingling sensation. The machine was hovering about thirty feet up. Tanner raised his AR-15 and let loose with an entire magazine. The rounds were blanks, all part of the show.

He pointed up and shouted. "See that? The damn thing has a force field around it."

His companion nodded in agreement and continued to stare at the lights in wonder. He had been eyeing Tanner with suspicion, but by attacking the weird object in the sky, Tanner had deflected the man's misgivings.

As he reloaded with live ammo, Tanner looked around and saw everyone gazing up at the "Flying Saucer", while others had left their positions to draw closer to the area beneath it. Tanner slipped off toward the rear of the property, as several men came out of the house. Among them was a man who wasn't buying it.

"It's a distraction, you idiots, not a fucking spaceship!"

There was an accented voice that carried a tone of disagreement, although Tanner couldn't make out all the words over the humming sound of the drone. He moved behind a metal dumpster that was itself behind a cinder block wall, then readied his remote.

Gunfire erupted. One gun at first, then several more as they shot at the UFO. The humming ceased, to be replaced by shouts of triumph and the crash of the drone. Then came silence.

Someone shouted excitedly in Spanish. "Aliens, look at that thing. It's an alien!"

Tanner smirked, apparently, the dummies were exposed amid the wreckage. A figure ran by, heard but not seen, followed by another. Two of the snipers, or maybe some of the foot patrol from the perimeter, whichever, were being drawn in toward the downed craft.

A voice shouted above the others. It was the same voice of reason that had claimed the UFO a fake.

"Stop staring at that pile of shit and look alert! This is a trick. Can't you see that? Now spread out or go back to your positions."

"Too late for that," Tanner said, as he pushed twice on the only red button on the remote. He had distracted the men and deflected any suspicion off himself. It was time to destroy.

The night filled with light once more as a brilliant flash appeared. It was accompanied by a tremendous blast of plastic explosives. The drone contained military-grade C-4 packed with ball bearings. Anyone who'd been standing near the downed drone was dead, and possibly shredded, while the columns at the front of the house collapsed into the circular driveway, crushing an ornate water fountain.

Debris pelted the wall Tanner was behind as the ground beneath him trembled. One of the ball bearings made it through the block wall and rang the side of the dumpster like a gong. Tanner's ears ached from the noise, but the ringing stopped by the time he entered the home from the rear.

He found no one on the lower floor, but then saw several men standing amid the debris at what had been the front of the house. They were either disoriented from the blast or marveling at the level of destruction. Tanner cut all but one of them down before they knew what was happening, while the last man went down while running.

Several of the men were still alive, but had suffered serious wounds. Whether they lived or died, Tanner didn't care. They were out of the fight, and his real target was to be found somewhere else inside the home.

The house had twenty-foot ceilings and a dramatic sweeping staircase made of marble. Debris from the partially collapsed roof littered the first few steps. Tanner jumped over it, crouched, and ran up the stairs while hugging the ornate and golden metal railing.

No one fired, and he reached the landing to begin searching the rooms. As he opened one door, a window exploded, and a round caught him in the chest, just below the top of his vest. The pain was epic. Tanner dragged himself away from the opening and looked for movement through watering eyes.

A sniper. One of the snipers was in the trees at the south side of the home. Tanner had opened the door while leaning over. The man must have taken his shot, while aiming at Tanner's head.

Tanner understood that if he'd not been trained to keep moving, constantly moving and bobbing during a search, and had stayed still after opening the door, his head would have been blown off.

Tanner recovered enough to roll past the doorway and, with greater caution, finished searching the floor. Moss Murphy was nowhere to be found, nor was Liam, and there was still a sniper to take care of. Tanner found the access to the roof in the form of a pull-down ladder in a hallway. He opened the hatch after darkening the hall, so no light would spill out, and after climbing up, he crawled to the edge of the roof.

A series of red & blue lights could be intermittently glimpsed in the distance through the trees, as the police and emergency services headed toward the scene. Tanner lay still and watched the area at the rear of the house. While it was possible that the sniper had stayed in position where he was, on the south side of the home, Tanner thought he would move toward the rear.

He would assume that Tanner would bolt from the property before the arrival of the authorities, and a smart man would head out the back, where there were no roads. A small town was six miles away in that direction. Once there, a car could be stolen, or a place could be found to hide out in.

As the sounds of sirens split the night, Tanner spotted the sniper. The shooter was a lighter man-shaped shadow against the darker shapes of the tree branches. Tanner took aim with the AR-15 and sent several rounds at the man.

A loud grunt was followed by a scream as the man fell to the ground. After reentering the house, Tanner shed his jacket to reveal the dark-blue uniform shirt of a cop. Once he turned the reversible jacket inside out, it too was dark-blue and had a phony badge on it.

A cap from beneath the shirt helped the look, along with a metal name tag and clip-on tie taken from a pocket. Finally, Tanner connected a police shoulder mic to his jacket, with the dangling cord hidden away down a sleeve.

His belt was missing all the standard police gear, but his silhouette read cop; it would be enough to get him off the property at night. Outside the house all was chaos, as the dead were many, and often in pieces. What wounded there were, were vocal, with most screaming.

One man, who'd only been slashed across the face by flying debris, was claiming that the aliens had attacked them and that someone needed to, "Alert the fucking Air Force."

Tanner slipped into the trees and a short while later five police cars came onto the property. Then came the ambulances, followed by the fire department, but by then, the fires had all burned themselves out.

Tanner left the trees and moved among the chaos. After watching the cops who'd arrived in a sixth vehicle disappear into the house, Tanner climbed in the cruiser they had left running.

The cop at the front gate just waved him on through while arguing with the driver of a news van who sought entrance onto the property.

Rounding a curve on the road, Tanner saw two more cops looking over his flatbed truck. He gave a little toot of his horn as he sent them a wave and kept driving.

When he was ten miles from the house, he stole a car from a movie theater parking lot after discarding the cop look and police cruiser. While sitting in a bar and nursing a beer, he pondered his next move.

Moss Murphy owned a restaurant in the heart of Boston. Perhaps he thought that being around so many people would protect him. If so, he was mistaken. Tanner went online and found out what he could about the eatery. It looked like it was going to be a long night of killing.

26
YOU DRIVE

SAMMY ACQUIRED A SECOND CAR FROM THE SAME SOURCE that had supplied the first vehicle. He was using it now as he wove up and down the rainy streets of Metairie, Louisiana, in a search pattern.

Along with the car, he'd asked for and received information. The cops had found the money Ricky had stolen. It was stashed inside his trailer, so that was gone forever.

Julie was being held over for arraignment and would face murder charges connected with Ricky Valente's death. Julie's stalker was named Victor Fenner. Fenner was in the hospital after being found shot twice. He was claiming he was the victim of an attempted carjacking, but Julie had placed suspicion on him.

However, Fenner was a solid citizen with no record, while Julie was an ex-con. Sammy was the only one who might be able to help Julie, but the cops wouldn't take his word for anything, not when his last name was Giacconi.

To his surprise, Sammy felt bad about Julie's predicament and wished he could help, but the best he could do was to pay for her lawyer when the time came to go to trial. Why he would do that much he had no idea. The woman was good-looking, sexy even, but he didn't think it was that. The women who worked at Johnny R's were just as beautiful, and a few of them had made it clear that they liked him. Sammy had ignored the attention and kept his mind on work.

Whatever it was about Julie, it had him out late roaming the streets during a rainstorm. When at last he'd found what, or rather whom, he'd been looking for, Sammy realized that was only half the battle.

It was Missy, Julie's runaway dog, who was pressed against the base of a palm tree. The hound was soaked to the skin and shivering either from the rain, fear, or a combination of both. To aid in his success, Sammy had stopped at a convenience store, where he'd bought dry dog food.

Although she seemed to remember him, Missy was reluctant to jump in Sammy's car until he shook the bag of kibble. Once he had her, he snuck her into his motel room and dried her off, then placed a blanket on the floor for her to lay on.

"What am I going to do with you if Julie goes to prison?"

Missy cocked her head, but had no answer to offer, and neither did Sammy.

IN NEW YORK CITY, SARA SAT OUT ON THE BALCONY OF the hotel suite she'd taken with Tanner and thought about her future. She was not the type to lay around for very long doing nothing, while she also enjoyed work that offered challenges. The FBI had fit that bill, but it also served-up mind-numbing periods where nothing happened, and then there was the drudgery of filling out official reports.

Working with Tanner had been the best job of her life, and while she loved him, neither of them wanted to work together on a regular basis. She needed her own arena to work in, one where she could excel, and yes, help people. Alicia was right. She had saved Kevin's life, along with Gabriel's, and the jittery Roland.

Killing Luis Zade hadn't bothered her at all. The son of a bitch had been willing to murder anyone who got between him and the bank money, and he would have come after her if she'd let him live.

There was that offer from Jacques Durand, but it required her to live abroad most of the time. Not only would that entail long absences from Tanner, but from New York City as well.

After Johnny Rossetti died, Sara thought she might never live in New York City ever again, but being back, she realized how wrong she'd been. She loved the city, and so did Tanner. It was their home.

When the idea struck her, it did so as she was dozing off to sleep with her feet up on the coffee table. Her bare feet hit the floor as she rose from her chair and paced along the railing of the balcony. After finding no flaw with the idea, she decided she would go ahead with it.

Sara Blake—Private Investigator. Yes, she liked the way that sounded. With her future path set, she left the balcony, crawled under the covers, and fell into a contented sleep.

TANNER ROLLED BY MOSS MURPHY'S SEAFOOD RESTAURANT and saw that it was closed and looked dark inside.

However, he spotted a car in the back corner of the parking lot with its interior brightly lit.

A second pass by the restaurant gave the impression of one occupant inside the vehicle. It was a male and he was seated in the driver's seat. Tanner ditched his stolen car several blocks from the restaurant and went to sniff out the trap.

Over an hour later, Tanner was convinced that there was no trap and wondered what the man was up to. The man in the car was Finn Kelly, and he appeared to be reading a book about boat building. Perhaps he had plans to sail back to Ireland.

Tanner approached the open window of the driver's side door and was gratified to see Finn Kelly tense as he spoke to him. "What game are you playing here?"

Finn turned and smiled at Tanner. "You're as good as they say. I can't remember the last time someone snuck up on me."

"Answer my question."

"I'm here to see that no more of my friends die while trying to stop you. I've heard reports of the devastation you caused at the house."

"If you want to kill me, Kelly, you're using an odd method to get there."

"I want to end this war, Tanner, not your life. I'm here to make a peace offering to Mr. Pullo."

"Moss Murphy sent you?"

The Irish lilt was strong in Kelly's next words and the gray eyes crinkled.

"Oh no, Mr. Moss Murphy did not send me on this errand. And I'll wager by now he wants me dead."

"Get to the bottom line."

"To do that, I'll have to open the trunk."

"Fine, step out of the car… but slowly."

Finn Kelly did as Tanner said and moved with deliberate intent. When he used the key to open the trunk, Tanner stood behind him. Once the trunk was sitting wide open, so were Tanner's eyes.

Liam Murphy lay inside the trunk bound, gagged, and unconscious.

"I spiked the little pisser's drink. He'll sleep all the way to New York City."

Tanner slammed the trunk, removed the keys from the lock, then handed them to Kelly.

"You drive."

27
NEVER ARRIVE EMPTY-HANDED

During the trip back to Manhattan, Tanner listened as Finn Kelly explained how the Boston mob was drawn into starting a war with the Giacconi Family.

"Liam back there in the trunk thinks he's a modern-day Lucky Luciano, only instead of uniting the Irish, Jewish, and Italian mobs, he was going to unite everyone. While he was in school in California he became friendly with a gang leader named Vincente Chavez. Chavez heads a street gang called the AK's, as in AK-47's. They have over a thousand members. Liam convinced Chavez that he could take down the Giacconi family and move his own people in there along with the AKs."

"His own people? What people?"

Finn smiled. "Yeah, see, the kid thinks he runs things, and his father lets him get away with it."

"You mean he sanctions it. Delusions of grandeur or not, these robberies and attacks wouldn't happen without Moss Murphy's say so."

"True, but that came later. In the beginning, it was just Liam and a few punks like that Sean O'Doyle. I began to suspect something was up and asked around, but Moss wasn't sure what was happening until you were attacked on the highway and O'Doyle's body was found with those gang members."

"That was when Liam brought his father into the loop?"

"Yeah, and by then, things were a mess. Still, the kid had shown that it was possible to hit the Giacconis and get away with it when he took the town of Killburry without a fight."

"That was Pullo showing respect to Moss Murphy by not killing his kid outright, but trust me, Joe wasn't about to give up territory."

"That was what I figured, and I told Moss as much. Anyway, when the hit on you went wrong, Moss knew he had entered a tunnel that had only one exit and that there was no way to turn around and go back. They had to kill you and Pullo, or they would be killed themselves."

"Murphy should have explained things to Joe. Liam is young enough that he would get a pass, for a price."

"We think alike Tanner, because again, that was my advice to Moss. But no, he listened to little Liam, and now his house is in shambles, men are dead, and he's in deep with the AKs."

"I'm not sure handing over Liam will stop the war."

"It stopped you. That's all I was after. If you kept going after Moss's hide tonight, more people would have died, and some of them are my friends."

"Going after Moss Murphy wasn't a contract. If it were, I'd kill him no matter what."

"I understand."

Tanner had informed Joe by text that he would be back in the city before dawn. To his surprise, he received a text back telling him that everyone was still at the club. Tanner had Kelly drive around to the rear of Johnny R's, where the limo sat. The metal beast was catching the first faint rays of daylight across its tinted glass.

Kelly pointed at the damage visible on the car's rear. "Pullo's chauffeur should be more careful."

"In more ways than one," Tanner said.

The rear door of the club opened and Pullo stepped out with Bosco and Rico. Seeing Finn Kelly standing beside Tanner made a look of surprise appear on each man's face.

Tanner jerked a thumb at Kelly. "He's with me."

"And like a good guest, I brought a gift along," Kelly said.

Later that morning in New Orleans, Sammy left Missy in his motel room while he went out to take care of a little unpleasant business. It was time to pay the snitch.

Being a disagreeable task even when things went well, having to hand over more money to resolve the Ricky Valente mess grated on Sammy. He was in the same trailer park where Ricky had died, and where Julie had lived like a hunted animal. The snitch's trailer was located at the edge of the main section and sat up higher than its neighbors.

Sammy's knocking on the thin metal door was answered by an old woman whose face broadcast her distrust of him. A former hooker, her beauty, if any, had long departed and left behind a wrinkled crone.

"If you're selling, I ain't buying."

"I'm here to pay you for the information you passed on to New York City."

"Huh? Oh! Wait, yes, yes, come right in. I should have pegged you for an errand boy, as young as you are."

Sammy stepped inside and saw the two cats at the same moment he smelled the odor of their litter box.

"I've been waiting for you to show up, and I'm so glad to see you're not the other guy."

"What other guy?"

The old woman smiled with one corner of her mouth as she made her fingers into a gun. It wasn't a good gun, because the fingers were crooked, but Sammy got the idea.

"You're talking about the shooter?"

"He gave me the creeps. But tell me something, why frame that girl? Did she screw with the Giacconis too?"

"You're saying you saw the hit go down?"

The lopsided smile appeared again, but this time it was accompanied by a wink. "I filmed it. I got him coming and going from both trailers. See, I placed a camera up on the roof of this thing, one of them little ones. That Ricky was worth money. I wasn't letting him pack up and leave without me knowing it."

Sammy stared at the old woman for a moment without saying anything. Was it possible he was going to be able to help Julie after all?

"I need to see this video, and I'll pay you for a copy."

"How much?"

"I'll give you five hundred, along with your payment."

This time the whole mouth smiled. "You can have it, but you know you can't do anything with it."

"What do you mean?"

"Think about it, boy. If you sold this to a TV station and they put it on the air, the man on the film would kill you too, or one of his friends, goombas they call them."

"You're right, but I still want a copy."

"Let's see the money."

Sammy handed her the envelope of cash he carried, then he pulled five-hundred from his wallet.

"Now, let's see this video."

Julie was in a jail cell, convinced she was going to prison for years. She had told her improbable story to half a dozen cops and an assistant DA and saw the disbelief in their eyes. When Fenner was found in the church parking lot with two wounded knees, one of the cops, a female detective, spoke with her again. She was a middle-aged woman who had grown hardened by her tough job, but not so callous that she didn't care about seeking the truth.

While talking to the female detective, Julie thought the woman might believe her, although she hadn't said so. But the woman seemed unsympathetic once she'd come back from visiting Victor Fenner in the hospital.

Victor Fenner. At last, Julie knew the name of her tormentor. But Fenner was respected by the cops, and was an investigator himself, although not a police officer.

Fenner's story of a carjacking rang false to the female detective, she admitted that much, but she hadn't been ready to accept Julie's tale of stalking without more evidence.

Meanwhile, the evidence that she killed Ricky Valente was enough to see her convicted. The court-appointed attorney was already talking about taking a plea bargain arrangement that would place her behind bars for many years. On top of everything else, Missy was gone off to who knew where and had spent the night out in a rainstorm.

Julie felt the tears welling up and this time she let them come. When the key turned in her cell door, it made her jump and she wiped at her wet face with her sleeve.

It was the female detective... and she was smiling.

"Wipe those eyes, girl. You're free to go."

"What?"

"Video evidence has come to light that all but shows Victor Fenner killing Ricky Valente. It damn sure shows him framing you."

Julie stood. "Are you serious?"

The detective grinned at her. "You're free, Julie, and you no longer have to look over your shoulder for Victor Fenner."

"Free," Julie whispered.

More tears came, but they were birthed by joy.

28
IT'S FOR YOU

Julie was released from jail, while arrangements were being made to move Fenner to a hospital ward. It was a move Fenner's lawyers were fighting, but the video evidence against him was damning. His veneer of normalcy had slipped when he'd been shown the video taken by the old woman. Knowing that Julie was out of his reach had enraged him so much that he slapped at the laptop displaying the video. After punching a nurse in the face, Fenner had to be tranquilized, and was being considered for a psych evaluation.

The female detective, whose name was Karla Cooper, had been kind enough to call around to animal shelters in the area where Missy had run off. She had no luck finding a dog matching Missy's description, and Julie planned to go looking for her dog.

She had nothing but the clothes on her back and her old car. Her rented trailer was part of Fenner's crime scene, since he had hidden the bloody sneakers and the murder weapon there. It would be another day until Julie could enter it again.

That didn't matter a damn to Julie. She was finally free of Victor Fenner's threats, although, she'd have to live with the results of his past actions. There was still no proof that Fenner had framed her for the charges that sent her to jail in California. Also, as a condition of the plea agreement, she had admitted her guilt in that case.

She was still banned from working as a nurse, and it was likely she always would be. Despite that, Julie was happy, and once she found Missy, she'd be able to move ahead in life without the shadow of Fenner clouding her days.

She was headed toward the bus stop when she spotted Sammy. She was going to catch a bus that would take her back to the trailer park, so she could get her car. Sammy was surprise enough, as Julie figured he had gone back to New York City, but she was shocked to see him holding Missy, and to her amazement, Missy was licking Sammy's hand. It seemed her dog had finally met a man she liked.

Julie ran to them and took Missy in her arms. "Oh, my baby. I thought I might never see you again."

"I knew you liked me," Sammy said.

Julie laughed. "I was talking to Missy, but I'm glad to see you too. How did you find her?"

"By looking for her. She spent the night in my motel room getting kibble all over the carpet."

Julie smiled at Sammy. "Thank you, that was very kind of you."

"Why don't we talk over lunch? It's my treat."

"Could we make it food from a drive-thru? I don't want to leave Missy alone for a while yet."

"I'll do better than that. Since it's a warm day, I'll get take-out from a restaurant and we'll eat in the park."

"Okay, but tell me something, is Sammy really your name?"

Sammy sighed inwardly, thinking his next words would scare Julie off, but he might as well get it out in the open. "I'm Sammy Giacconi."

"That name sounds familiar, especially when I connect it to New York."

"My grandfather was Sam Giacconi. You might have heard of him."

Sammy knew Julie remembered the name when her eyes went wide. "The Giacconi Family... and you're a member?"

"In good standing, and I'll understand if you don't want that lunch anymore."

Julie nibbled her bottom lip. "You came down here to kill Shane, I mean Ricky, and get back that money you told me about?"

"I did."

Julie studied Sammy's face. "Are you always so sad? You look so sad at times."

"Um, I lost someone. I guess I'm still—what about lunch?"

"Only if we get shrimp somewhere. I have such a craving for shrimp."

"Deal," Sammy said.

AS PLANNED, THEY ATE IN THE PARK AT A PICNIC TABLE while Missy sniffed trees and rolled atop the grass. Sammy mostly listened, as Julie relayed how good it felt to have Fenner behind her and lamented the loss of her nursing career.

Sammy excused himself and made a call while Julie cleaned the table and deposited the debris from their lunch in a nearby trashcan. When she sat across from Sammy again, he handed her his phone.

"I have someone who'd like to talk to you."

"Who?"

"She'll explain."

Julie reached over tentatively, then placed the phone to her ear as if the sound of an air horn might emanate from the tiny speaker.

"Hello?"

"Hello, Julie, my name is Laurel Pullo."

Julie talked to Laurel for over twenty minutes. When the conversation ended, she told Sammy she wanted to go to New York City with him.

"Well, not *with* you, not like that, I mean, together, but like on the same plane."

"Right," Sammy said. "And I'm glad about it. You'll get a fresh start."

"Thank you for connecting me with Laurel. She sounds great."

"She is."

Missy walked over and put her front paws on Sammy's leg, asking to be picked up.

Sammy lifted the dog onto his lap and petted her behind the ears. "Missy is a good dog."

"Yes," Julie said, "and maybe a good judge of character too."

29
THAT FIRST STEP IS A DOOZY

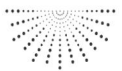

Gina Rossetti and Liam Murphy were seated beside each other in a pair of straight back chairs that were positioned in front of Joe Pullo's desk.

Tanner and Finn Kelly were present, along with Bosco. Liam had elbowed Bosco in the ribs, in an attempt to escape. Bosco put a stop to that by jamming his fingers hard against the nerve cluster in Liam's shoulder, which made the punk cry out in pain.

Gina, with a bruise on her chin, gazed over at Joe with defiance, while Liam's cocky look never wavered. Bosco and Kelly stood on either side of Joe, with Bosco on his right. Tanner was positioned just behind Liam's chair, in case the boy needed a reminder to behave.

"Hey Finn, my old man is going to have you sliced into fish bait."

Kelly ignored him and took out a throwaway phone. He had texted Moss Murphy and let him know that they needed to set up a secure line for communication. Murphy, or one of his people, texted Kelly back minutes later with a time, a phone number, and a method to use.

"Mr. Pullo, once I get Moss on the line I'll place the call on speakerphone."

"Do that. He'll need to hear from all of us."

The call was answered swiftly. Kelly activated the speakerphone and Moss Murphy's voice filled the room while in mid-sentence.

"—do with my kid? So help me, Kelly, if that boy is dead I'll not only kill you, but I'll hunt down your family back in Ireland as well."

"Liam is still in one piece, Moss. He's in New York City with Mr. Pullo, Tanner, myself, and Pullo's man, Bosco. There's also a lovely young lass named Gina Rossetti. Apparently, she was Liam's informant."

"A girl? He was making major moves based on information from a girl?"

"She's smart, Dad. She was the one who came up with the idea to use the gas at the bakery."

"Liam? Boy, are you all right?"

"Not a hair out of place. And don't give in, you hear me? Pullo knows that if he so much as touches me there will be hell to pay."

"You're damn right there will be hell to pay. Pullo! Joe? You there? Say something."

"You're gonna give me what I want, Moss, or else. There's no need for me to spell it out."

The line was silent, then came the sound of a throat clearing. "I understand you're soon to be a father yourself, Joe. I'm sure there's no need for me to spell out what *I* mean by that."

"Murphy, this is Tanner. You're going to beg Joe to forgive you for what you just said, or the next sound you hear is your son's right arm breaking."

"He threatened my boy, Tanner. Two can play that game."

"Your *boy* is a man and a member of organized crime. And Murphy, I do not bluff."

"Put a leash on Tanner, Joe, then we can talk."

Tanner grabbed Liam's right wrist with one hand and raised the arm high, while pushing on his shoulder to keep him in the chair. Tanner then brought Liam's forearm down in a blur, where it collided with his rising knee.

There was an audible *Crack!* which was followed by Liam screaming, as he gazed in horror at his misshapen arm.

Seated beside Liam, Gina Rossetti was making a face of disgust, as she leaned away from her lover.

"He broke my arm! Dad, Tanner broke my arm! Oh, damn it hurts like a motherfucker."

"Tanner, you son of a bitch! You touch my boy again and there will be nowhere you can hide."

"Hide? Murphy, that was me at your house last night, remember? You threw your best at me and I tore it to shreds. Joe better start hearing a tone of respect coming out of your mouth or next time I won't stop until you and your kid are dead."

There came the sound of labored breathing amid muttered curses as Moss Murphy tried to control his temper. When he spoke again, he sounded calm.

"Pullo… tell me what you want."

"I want twenty-five million dollars."

"Are you insane? Where do you get that figure from?"

"I like the sound of it. Give me your decision. Liam or the money; you can't have both."

"This is blackmail!"

Liam leaned toward the phone and shouted. "Send a fucking army here, Dad, our people, the AKs, some mercs. Use that twenty-five million to put Tanner and Pullo in the ground."

"That is an option, Pullo. Liam's right. I could do that."

"You could, but your boy would be dead. It's Liam or the money."

"Fuck that! How about you send Liam back here now or I use those millions to hire that army."

Tanner cocked his head as he looked down at the phone. "Joe, I think Murphy can't grasp the concept of his boy dying. I would like to change that."

Joe stared up at Tanner. He had no idea what Tanner might do, but he knew Liam wouldn't like it.

"Do what you think is best, Tanner."

Liam was yanked from his seat by his hair as Tanner gripped his broken arm. The pain made the young thug weak, and he cried out in agony. Tanner left the office while dragging Liam along, as he headed to the left of the elevators.

There was a staircase there consisting of eighteen blue concrete steps with a black metal handrail above them. The stairs were brilliantly lit by fluorescent lighting, which reflected off the surrounding cinder block walls that were painted a stark white. Without any preamble or warning, Tanner tossed Liam Murphy down the stairs, headfirst.

Liam screamed while instinctively stretching out his arms to brace for impact. When his right hand collided with a step, a piece of bone from his broken arm tore through his skin. After flipping over, Liam's left leg slammed hard against the edge of a step. The sound of the thigh bone breaking was as loud as the snapping of a tree branch. As he neared the bottom of the steps, Liam received a nasty slash across his handsome face when his head collided with the edge of the handrail.

Lying at the bottom of the stairs in what could only be described as a broken, bloody heap, Liam Murphy moaned and whimpered. Joe, along with the others, had followed Tanner. Joe held the phone out, so Moss Murphy could hear Liam's plaintive cries of pain.

Finn Kelly took a photo of Liam. "I'll send this to Moss," he said.

Tanner stared at Gina Rossetti with the full force of his intense gaze. She had set him up to be killed when he was attacked while driving the van.

"I should toss you down there too."

Gina shook her head in a frantic motion as she imagined tumbling down those stairs. She moved closer to Joe, as if for protection. Joe shoved her toward Bosco.

"Put her back in her chair."

Gina went with Bosco without complaint. Anything to get away from those stairs, and Tanner.

Moss Murphy's voice echoed in the hallway as he spoke in a mournful tone. "Oh, my boy, Tanner, what the fuck did you do to my boy?"

"I tossed him down a flight of stairs and I can drag him back up here and do it again. Now, tell us more about that army you're going to send here."

"Is he, oh God. Liam! Can you hear me, boy?"

A weak voice answered, echoing in the hallway, and there was no doubt its owner was racked with pain.

"Pay him… pay him anything… any, oh, oh God it hurts."

"Call an ambulance, Pullo!"

"Ambulances cost money," Tanner said.

"I'll pay, you fucker. I'll pay Pullo his damn twenty-five million, but so help me God, Pullo, and you too, Tanner, there will be a reckoning someday."

"Kelly will call you back with the transfer details," Joe said.

"Whatever, just get my boy to a doctor."

Rico Nazario was down in the club. Joe took out his own phone and called him. Rico was to have Red help him ferry Liam to the clinic. Having overheard one side of the short conversation, Moss Murphy protested that idea.

"Clinic? I want Liam taken to the best hospital in New York."

"Goodbye, Moss," Joe said. After ending the call, Pullo broke the burner phone in half and tossed the pieces onto Liam. "Now it's time to deal with Gina."

"I can wait out in the reception area if you'd like?" Kelly said to Joe.

"No, come back in the office. You might as well view our dirty laundry too."

Gina had regained her composure, or at least its appearance, because she greeted Joe with a smile.

"Thank you."

"For what?" Joe said.

"For helping me to see how Liam was just using me."

"Was it the same way you used Red?"

"Red?"

"Andre, that's his nickname."

"Oh, and yeah, I used him, but I did it for Liam."

Joe leaned back in his seat and stared at Gina. While Pullo's gaze was in no way as intense as Tanner's, it was still unnerving. Joe pointed at Tanner. "You tried to have Tanner killed and set the lot of us up to be murdered. If you weren't Johnny Rossetti's kid sister you'd be dead already."

"What are you going to do to me?"

"I'm going to give you a choice. Leave here and go out on your own, or head to Vegas where you'll be given a job in your Uncle Al's old casino."

Gina made a face of disgust. "I never liked fat old Uncle Al, but I do like Vegas. What sort of job is it?"

"They'll decide that when you get there, but understand something, if I ever see you in New York City again that will be the day you die."

Gina opened her mouth to protest, but then thought better of it. "I'll go to Vegas. How long will it take until my car is fixed?"

Bosco chuckled at Gina's nerve, then said, "Unbelievable."

"The car stays here. You'll be taking the bus."

"A bus? All the way to Las Vegas?"

"I can think of a shorter trip," Tanner said. "That one involves a distance of only six feet, straight down."

Gina clutched her throat as she leaned away from Tanner. "How soon can I go?"

"Today," Joe said. "Bosco here will drive you to the bus station."

"I have to pack first, and I'll need money to start over."

"Don't push me, Gina. I loved Johnny like a brother, but don't push me."

Gina shut up, and Bosco told her to come with him. With both chairs empty in front of the desk, Tanner sat to Joe's left, while Finn Kelly settled in Gina's vacated seat.

"What are your plans, Kelly?" Joe asked.

"Well now, I've burned all the bridges that lead back to Boston. Maybe I'll go freelance."

"There's a place for you here if you want it."

"You're serious?"

"I already have a right-hand man. That's Bosco, who is an Underboss and a Consigliere rolled into one. He's been handling the load well and making no complaints about it. But you could take some of the workload off Bosco and he could have a life again. I also need someone to sniff out trouble like Liam Murphy before it gets out of hand. Along with that, I'll be bringing in some fresh blood, a guy like you can make sure we get the cream of the crop."

"I accept the offer, Mr. Pullo, pending the financial arrangements of course."

"Call me Joe, and thanks for what you did today. I know your reasons had nothing to do with helping out the Giacconi Family, but that was the result, and it took guts."

Tanner stood and stretched his neck. "I'll be at the hotel, Joe."

"All right, and get some sleep. I think we could all use some. But give me a call tomorrow night and I'll have that apartment you and Sara need."

"Make it something up high, Sara likes a view."

Joe smiled. "You won't be disappointed."

30

MANHATTAN'S HIT MAN

The following day, Sammy escorted Julie to the club right from the airport. Johnny R's wouldn't be open for hours and only Red was at the bar, where he sipped on a soda.

Laurel met with Julie inside Joe's office, and she and Julie seemed to get along well. Julie had come to New York City to work at the Giacconi's illegal clinic and would be doing the work she loved, nursing.

After her talk with Laurel, Julie took the elevator down to the bar where Sammy was talking to Ivanov. At Sammy's feet, Missy was eating chicken scraps from the kitchen.

"How did you and Laurel get along?"

"Great, and I start tomorrow."

"That's good," Sammy said, and found himself becoming lost in Julie's eyes.

Julie raised herself up on her toes and kissed Sammy on the mouth. When they parted, Sammy was smiling.

Up in the office, Joe gazed out through the one-way glass, saw Sammy's smile, and grinned a smile of his own.

"Laurel, you like this girl, Julie?"

"She's sweet, and I think she'll be great at the clinic. She has experience with gunshot wounds, having worked in Los Angeles."

"Yeah," Joe said. "I think she may be just what we need around here."

∼

That night, while having dinner at Martha Maglione's restaurant, Tanner and Sara discussed the recent events in their lives.

"The drug dealer that Professor Seagate wanted to frame for bank robbery was being murdered at about the same time Luis Zade was killing Seagate. The drug dealer had made an enemy while in prison. When that man was released, he tracked the drug dealer down and stabbed him to death. Ian Seagate's entire plan was for nothing."

"Kevin Kincaid was lucky you got involved," Tanner said. "I think you'll make a great P.I."

After finishing his lasagna, Tanner sipped wine while gazing out the restaurant's windows, at the lights of Broadway.

"Joe thinks that the Giacconis will be at war with some group or another for years to come, and he's right. There's a lot of competition out there for who will run the illegal trade in this city."

"I know from my time at the Bureau that the Mafia is in decline everywhere. Only Pullo seems to have stayed in control of his territory, and you're a big part of that."

"That's what Joe said too. It's why he was so generous with my compensation for dealing with Moss Murphy."

Sara grinned. "About that, let's go get a look at what he gave you. I hope it fits us, otherwise we'll have to sell it."

"From everything he told me about it, I think you'll love it."

A SHORT TIME LATER, TANNER AND SARA GAZED OUT AT the city from the terrace of a condo on the Westside of Manhattan.

The home's features included views to the North, South, East, and West. It had over 4000 sq. ft., which included 6 bedrooms, 6 bathrooms, 1 powder room, a 5-star chef's kitchen, and it was all perched atop the 65th floor. The home's huge windows granted spectacular views of the city's skyline, Central Park, and the Hudson River.

A feature that pleased Tanner was the separate entrance. It came complete with its own elevator, which connected the home's owner with a private garage, so that their comings and goings could remain unobserved by the building's other residents.

Sara had been wandering through the home for nearly an hour and her mouth was still opened in shock.

"Pullo just gave you this?"

"It's payment for services rendered, plus, I'll be on retainer for a year."

"This must be worth ten million."

"More than that, but don't worry, Joe recently came into some money."

"What about the Condo Board? Don't we have to be interviewed?"

"Yes, but Joe says it will be a formality."

Sara turned and hugged him. "Considering who you are, can we really live here?"

"Thomas Myers is clean on paper, and he's always had a good income."

"This place is so beautiful. It's like a palace. And this view, I've never seen one better."

"So, we keep it?"

Sara grinned. "Yes."

"All right, and just to be safe, I want to transfer the deed to you soon."

"Why?"

"Thomas Myers is an alias. If it gets burned, you won't have to give this place up."

"Still, Tanner, to just hand me this, this… mansion in the sky, it's too much."

Tanner kissed her. "We'll figure something out. Now all you need to do is find an office for your P.I. business."

Sara laughed. "I'll be the only private investigator who lives in a place like this."

Tanner hugged Sara from behind and kissed the top of her head.

"I guess we're home."

TANNER RETURNS!

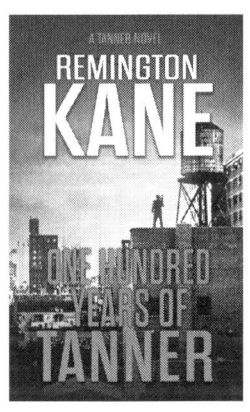

ONE HUNDRED YEARS OF TANNER - BOOK 19

AFTERWORD

Thank you,

REMINGTON KANE

JOIN MY INNER CIRCLE

You'll receive FREE books, such as,

SLAY BELLS – A TANNER NOVEL – BOOK 0

TAKEN! ALPHABET SERIES – 26 ORIGINAL TAKEN! TALES

BLUE STEELE - KARMA

Also – Exclusive short stories featuring TANNER, along with other books.

TO BECOME AN INNER CIRCLE MEMBER, GO TO:
http://remingtonkane.com/mailing-list/

ALSO BY REMINGTON KANE

The TANNER Series in order

INEVITABLE I - A Tanner Novel - Book 1

KILL IN PLAIN SIGHT - A Tanner Novel - Book 2

MAKING A KILLING ON WALL STREET - A Tanner Novel - Book 3

THE FIRST ONE TO DIE LOSES - A Tanner Novel - Book 4

THE LIFE & DEATH OF CODY PARKER - A Tanner Novel - Book 5

WAR - A Tanner Novel- A Tanner Novel - Book 6

SUICIDE OR DEATH - A Tanner Novel - Book 7

TWO FOR THE KILL - A Tanner Novel - Book 8

BALLET OF DEATH - A Tanner Novel - Book 9

MORE DANGEROUS THAN MAN - A Tanner Novel - Book 10

TANNER TIMES TWO - A Tanner Novel - Book 11

OCCUPATION: DEATH - A Tanner Novel - Book 12

HELL FOR HIRE - A Tanner Novel - Book 13

A HOME TO DIE FOR - A Tanner Novel - Book 14

FIRE WITH FIRE - A Tanner Novel - Book 15

TO KILL A KILLER - A Tanner Novel - Book 16

WHITE HELL – A Tanner Novel - Book 17

MANHATTAN HIT MAN – A Tanner Novel - Book 18

ONE HUNDRED YEARS OF TANNER – A Tanner Novel -

Book 19

REVELATIONS - A Tanner Novel - Book 20

THE SPY GAME - A Tanner Novel - Book 21

A VICTIM OF CIRCUMSTANCE - A Tanner Novel - Book 22

A MAN OF RESPECT - A Tanner Novel - Book 23

THE MAN, THE MYTH - A Tanner Novel - Book 24

ALL-OUT WAR - A Tanner Novel - Book 25

THE REAL DEAL - A Tanner Novel - Book 26

WAR ZONE - A Tanner Novel - Book 27

ULTIMATE ASSASSIN - A Tanner Novel - Book 28

KNIGHT TIME - A Tanner Novel - Book 29

PROTECTOR - A Tanner Novel - Book 30

BULLETS BEFORE BREAKFAST - A Tanner Novel - Book 31

VENGEANCE - A Tanner Novel - Book 32

TARGET: TANNER - A Tanner Novel - Book 33

BLACK SHEEP - A Tanner Novel - Book 34

FLESH AND BLOOD - A Tanner Novel - Book 35

NEVER SEE IT COMING - A Tanner Novel - Book 36

MISSING - A Tanner Novel - Book 37

CONTENDER - A Tanner Novel - Book 38

TO SERVE AND PROTECT - A Tanner Novel - Book 39

STALKING HORSE - A Tanner Novel - Book 40

THE EVIL OF TWO LESSERS - A Tanner Novel - Book 41

SINS OF THE FATHER AND MOTHER - A Tanner Novel - Book 42

SOULLESS - A Tanner Novel - Book 43

The Young Guns Series in order

YOUNG GUNS

YOUNG GUNS 2 - SMOKE & MIRRORS

YOUNG GUNS 3 - BEYOND LIMITS

YOUNG GUNS 4 - RYKER'S RAIDERS

YOUNG GUNS 5 - ULTIMATE TRAINING

YOUNG GUNS 6 - CONTRACT TO KILL

YOUNG GUNS 7 - FIRST LOVE

YOUNG GUNS 8 - THE END OF THE BEGINNING

A Tanner Series in order

TANNER: YEAR ONE

TANNER: YEAR TWO

TANNER: YEAR THREE

TANNER: YEAR FOUR

TANNER: YEAR FIVE

The TAKEN! Series in order

TAKEN! - LOVE CONQUERS ALL - Book 1

TAKEN! - SECRETS & LIES - Book 2

TAKEN! - STALKER - Book 3

TAKEN! - BREAKOUT! - Book 4

TAKEN! - THE THIRTY-NINE - Book 5

TAKEN! - KIDNAPPING THE DEVIL - Book 6

TAKEN! - HIT SQUAD - Book 7

TAKEN! - MASQUERADE - Book 8

TAKEN! - SERIOUS BUSINESS - Book 9

TAKEN! - THE COUPLE THAT SLAYS TOGETHER - Book 10

TAKEN! - PUT ASUNDER - Book 11

TAKEN! - LIKE BOND, ONLY BETTER - Book 12

TAKEN! - MEDIEVAL - Book 13

TAKEN! - RISEN! - Book 14

TAKEN! - VACATION - Book 15

TAKEN! - MICHAEL - Book 16

TAKEN! - BEDEVILED - Book 17

TAKEN! - INTENTIONAL ACTS OF VIOLENCE - Book 18

TAKEN! - THE KING OF KILLERS – Book 19

TAKEN! - NO MORE MR. NICE GUY - Book 20 & the Series Finale

The MR. WHITE Series

PAST IMPERFECT - MR. WHITE - Book 1

HUNTED - MR. WHITE - Book 2

The BLUE STEELE Series in order

BLUE STEELE - BOUNTY HUNTER- Book 1

BLUE STEELE - BROKEN- Book 2

BLUE STEELE - VENGEANCE- Book 3

BLUE STEELE - THAT WHICH DOESN'T KILL ME- Book 4

BLUE STEELE - ON THE HUNT- Book 5

BLUE STEELE - PAST SINS - Book 6

BLUE STEELE - DADDY'S GIRL - Book 7 & the Series Finale

The CALIBER DETECTIVE AGENCY Series in order

CALIBER DETECTIVE AGENCY - GENERATIONS- Book 1

CALIBER DETECTIVE AGENCY - TEMPTATION- Book 2

CALIBER DETECTIVE AGENCY - A RANSOM PAID IN BLOOD- Book 3

CALIBER DETECTIVE AGENCY - MISSING- Book 4

CALIBER DETECTIVE AGENCY - DECEPTION- Book 5

CALIBER DETECTIVE AGENCY - CRUCIBLE- Book 6

CALIBER DETECTIVE AGENCY – LEGENDARY – Book 7

CALIBER DETECTIVE AGENCY – WE ARE GATHERED HERE TODAY - Book 8

CALIBER DETECTIVE AGENCY - MEANS, MOTIVE, and OPPORTUNITY - Book 9 & the Series Finale

THE TAKEN!/TANNER Series in order

THE CONTRACT: KILL JESSICA WHITE - Taken!/Tanner - Book 1

UNFINISHED BUSINESS – Taken!/Tanner – Book 2

THE ABDUCTION OF THOMAS LAWSON - Taken!/Tanner – Book 3

PREDATOR - Taken!/Tanner - Book 4

DETECTIVE PIERCE Series in order

MONSTERS - A Detective Pierce Novel - Book 1

DEMONS - A Detective Pierce Novel - Book 2

ANGELS - A Detective Pierce Novel - Book 3

THE OCEAN BEACH ISLAND Series in order

THE MANY AND THE ONE - Book 1

SINS & SECOND CHANES - Book 2

DRY ADULTERY, WET AMBITION -Book 3

OF TONGUE AND PEN - Book 4

ALL GOOD THINGS… - Book 5

LITTLE WHITE SINS - Book 6

THE LIGHT OF DARKNESS - Book 7

STERN ISLAND - Book 8 & the Series Finale

THE REVENGE Series in order

JOHNNY REVENGE - The Revenge Series - Book 1

THE APPOINTMENT KILLER - The Revenge Series - Book 2

AN I FOR AN I - The Revenge Series - Book 3

ALSO

THE EFFECT: Reality is changing!

THE FIX-IT MAN: A Tale of True Love and Revenge

DOUBLE OR NOTHING

PARKER & KNIGHT

REDEMPTION: Someone's taken her

DESOLATION LAKE

TIME TRAVEL TALES & OTHER SHORT STORIES

MANHATTAN HIT MAN
Copyright © REMINGTON KANE, 2017
YEAR ZERO PUBLISHING

This book is a work of fiction. Names, characters, places and incidents either are products of the author's imagination or are used fictitiously.

Any resemblance to actual events or locales or persons, living or dead, is entirely coincidental.

All rights reserved. Except as permitted under the U.S. Copyright Act of 1976, no part of this publication may be reproduced, distributed or transmitted in any form or by any means, or stored in a database or retrieval system, without the prior written permission of the publisher.

 Created with Vellum

Printed in Great Britain
by Amazon